No Tears for Destiny

Mike Herd

This is an entirely fictional account of an imagined future scenario facing an independent Scotland. All names and characters in this book are fictitious and any similarity to any living person is accidental.

Also by the author

Sea Lavender
Niobium
Justice for Lydia
No Tears for Destiny
The Medusa Shield
The Spirit of Askival

No Tears for Destiny

"Hello my little precious darlings how are we all today? You're looking gorgeous."

"Mum stop being soppy, the neighbours might hear you."

"They like me talking to them look at those colours, I wish I could hug you all but you're only delicate little things."

Emlyn disliked being in the greenhouse it was too claustrophobic. It wasn't just the mass of growing flowers taking up most of the space it was because of the heavy cloying atmosphere they were exuding.

"What kind of job is it?" asked Mrs Llewellyn catching him off guard. She stopped watering and glanced at him as if to underline the question hanging in the air.

"I don't know exactly," he said hesitantly. "It depends on which department I end up in if I get the job that is."

"They didn't give you a job description? That's odd," she said putting the watering can down and picked up the secateurs.

Emlyn pulled a face as his mother leaned forward to nip a few dead leaves and at the same time sniff at a vibrant red carnation. He ran his fingers through his hair and stuck his hands in his jeans, sighing.

"Alright," she said with a grin. "I'm sure you'll tell me all about it in your own time, I know you must be a little nervous about the interview."

"It's not an interview it's more like a civil service entry exam," he said looking away. "I'll probably not get through anyway."

"Well wear something smart, first impressions and all that, it's so important."

"Yes mum."

There was a terrible sense of foreboding that was all too familiar. The pungent smell of fear was enhanced by the ominous silence and then it all began like a piece of theatre but in slow motion. A massive explosion shook the building as a gable end fell away letting in daylight streaming through clouds of dust. There was that silence again and then filtering through the ringing tones of tinnitus were shouts and machine gun fire. A body released an arc of blood trailing behind as it was thrown across what was left of an Iraqi class room. The surprise still registered on his face as he disappeared into the dust cloud. An incoming RPG exploded causing a pinging sound as the shrapnel bounced off the remaining walls. Then he heard the unmistakable sound of an Agusta Westland Apache attack helicopter and its M230, 30mm cannon fire. The dust cleared and incoming fire ceased. All around him were dead bodies covered in dust. Colin Alexander Reid screamed and woke up drenched in sweat. The nightmares varied in the levels of horror played out but this one was particularly bad. Shaking, he swung his legs out of the bed and sat there crying. He started breathing slowly and deliberately in the knowledge that it would eventually pass, until the next time.

Emlyn Llewellyn looked around the auditorium. It was like a small cinema with side ledges attached to the chairs. The women chosen to attend the examination seemed to be picked for their plainness. He sighed it was just like being back at Uni except the people who clearly didn't know each other and were all spread out, looked more diverse in age, gender and culture but there was a kind of similarity, no...more like a watermark of potentiality and enthusiasm running through each one like a stick of rock. It had been tough leaving home not because he was homesick but because he hated lying to his mother. He had been told in blunt terms that no one must know of the examination and so he hoped, that his mumblings skirting round the real reason for him going to London, had worked. He didn't realize that his mother was sensible enough not to press him. Excited and nervous at the same time he was willing all this to be over soon, when the door opened and in came a slim attractive young woman in a Harris Tweed waisted jacket, matching skirt and pale cream silk shirt. The murmur of sound stopped. She put her tablet on a desk folded her arms and gazed up at the assembled crowd walking forward with a clicking of her high heels on the parquetry wooden floor. Her eyes examined each and every face in turn causing a tense atmosphere. Some held her gaze others looked away. Emlyn was fascinated.

"You have all passed the online aptitude test..." Her words released the tension like a burst balloon. "...otherwise you wouldn't be here. Likewise you have all scored well in the three tests, The Verbal Reasoning Test that targets your speed, accuracy, reading comprehension, and language fluency. The Situational Judgement Test (SJT) to assess your actions and reactions in the workplace. And the Numerical Reasoning Test which as the name implies, assesses basic mathematical skills. You have a tablet that has been pre-programmed with the examination. It is not a question and answer test but various scenarios of which there may be one or two correct outcomes You will have thirty minutes to complete them and I should warn you that the pass rate is 100%." There was an audible gasp from the examinees. "This is about problem solving and lateral thinking. Any incorrect outcomes means you will have failed to progress to training with the Secret Intelligence Service. There are no trick puzzles and questions; you must use your intelligence, common sense and logic. The timing is intentionally pressurized because that's what happens in the world you wish to enter, good luck, your time starts now."

"What did you vote?" asked Jenny.

As they walked, seagulls circled above them against a leaden sky and called noisily as if wanting to be fed then they flew off.

"What do you think?" asked Paula in reply inhaling a cigarette.

Paula blew out the smoke turning her head as it came back in her face, her pony tail catching her eye. Walking home from the polling station they quickened their step against a cold wind funnelled by the River Tay slicing its way through Perth. Resignation followed her like an unwelcome companion cloaked in apathy and symptomatic of poverty. She was in her late fifties but looked more like early sixties and had that weariness women have when life has been hard but she still managed to find a spark of defiance to keep her spirit alive. She was too absorbed with day to day challenges to have time to reflect on where her life was heading. For her it had always been so and who knows maybe that would never change even under an independent Scotland.

"Me too," said Jenny.

She had always kept a sisterly eye over Paula who lived nearby. After Jenny's grandmother died she had moved into the flat that she had bought for her before her illness, now it was hers. Sometimes the port wine stain on the lower part of Jenny's cheek and neck reddened when she was angry or lost confidence. Now it was hardly noticeable through the skilful application of cosmetics. Her posture was striking in contrast to Paula's slight stoop. She walked along with an upright, straight back, shopping bag handles hooked over her shoulder occasionally slowing down to allow Paula to catch up. Jenny managed to get a hankie out of her bag in time and sneezed into it wiping her nose.

"It was busy in the community hall. Fancy having to wait all that time to vote," said Jenny stuffing her hankie up her sleeve. "I read that a huge amount of Scottish land has anonymous owners hiding their wealth and assets in offshore companies paying no tax. What's that all about?"

"I've always had a problem hiding my assets," said Paula drily.

"No seriously I hope an independent Scotland if we ever get one will sort that out."

"You'll never be able to do anything about that."

"I don't know. Maybe if there was a real land registry and the genuine owners were forced to claim ownership that could be a start."

"How would you get someone like that to declare the property and land that they own?"

"If they didn't turn up and make their claim showing proof, well then the land and buildings would revert to the Scottish Government. Why can't people in power see that? For the life of me I can't understand why normal people would want to vote no to independence," said Jenny.

Paula grunted. "Well you've hit the nail on the head. The haves would vote no. They're terrified of losing what they have, power, wealth, land, influence and media to control us haven'ts...telling us what to think. We've got nothing to lose and everything to gain. Let's face it, things couldn't get much worse. Can't remember the last time I bought a newspaper, a look at the front pages is enough. Social media that's where you find the truth."

"Social media? I didn't know you could afford broadband Paula."

"I can't. Anyway I don't need to there's a hotspot near enough to the flat, saves a fortune. Aye things'll be different come the revolution."

"Don't tell me you're a closet communist," Jenny laughed.

"Closet communist says you talking about land reform. Communism what does that mean anymore? I'm everything and anything depending on the question. But I'll tell you what I am right now, tired. I was hoping you had your car, what's wrong with it this time?"

Jenny tightened the red scarf around her neck. "I'm frightened I get stopped by the police. I don't know if it's roadworthy. Anyway I couldn't remember if there was a steep enough hill nearby."

"Not the starter motor again? I thought Colin fixed it."

"Yeah sure if you call banging it with a big hammer fixing it. He says it keeps sticking. Can't afford a new starter motor."

"New car is what you need more like, you can pay it on the never. Who buys a car with cash these days? There's a rumour going round that your steering's hopeless. You can only turn left handed corners."

Jenny laughed. "There's nothing wrong with it once it's going. You should learn to drive. I'll teach you."

"What in your car? No thanks I'll just keep cadging lifts."

"I wish I had taken it now my feet's killing me. It was busy today."

"You're lucky you've got a proper job in the supermarket not like me. Fifteen hours a week at the petrol station on the minimum wage, the bunch of cheap skates. I don't even get the living wage and that's a laugh as well, it should be called the existing wage because it's not a life it's an existence. I don't know though it could be worse I suppose, could be on zero hour's contract just being called in when they're busy and getting a bollocking if I don't pick up the phone...oh look out here's Joyce."

A heavily pregnant woman emerged from the baker shop carrying a see through bag of rolls. She unhooked the lead of her Jack Russell from a restricted parking sign post as he danced around her feet in pleasure, yapping.

"How are you Joyce it must be getting near?"

"Weary very weary. Everything is an effort. I'm overdue. This one'll probably be late for everything he's already late for his birthday."

Joyce a near neighbour of Paula's was slightly out of breath, her voice barely audible above the yapping dog.

"Quiet Benji. I think he knows there's going to be an addition to the family. He gets jealous of our youngest as it is. Can you wait for me I need to pick up something from the chemist?"

"Sorry Joyce I have to get home for Robbie, pop in for a cuppa when you get back."

They carried on up the hill towards the estate.

"It would take us all day to walk home with Joyce. Just a minute." Paula stopped and picked up fifty pence from the kerb. "Waste not want not how's Colin, I haven't seen him for a while?"

"He's not great. He's in Glasgow staying with his folks. He has an appointment with a therapist."

"Don't they have therapists in Perth?"

"She's a specialist."

Paula sighed. "I had a message from the care home. Mum keeps trying to escape. They found her wandering about in the high street with her nightie on. She said she was canvassing for independence. I don't know what to do."

"There's nothing you can do Paula except hope that we don't become like that."

They passed the bookies and a newspaper shop and narrowly avoiding a young boy riding his bike on the pavement. Paula shouted after him angrily.

"Just wait till I speak to your mother Garry Thomson. He'll come a cropper one day," she said shaking her fist. "So you've never actually said and I don't like to pry but what is it that's wrong with Colin?"

"He gets angry for no reason. It's something to do with his time in Iraq he doesn't like speaking about it. He'll not vote he hates politics and politicians. Anyway who's looking after Robbie?"

"Himself hopefully. He's twelve after all...I know, I don't like him going home to an empty flat but I have to work. It wasn't like that when we were kids. You weren't born then. Work was easy to come by, proper well paid work. It meant that my father could support my mother so that she could stay at home looking after us. Not like now. It's been hard since Robbie's father died. Are you going to stay up and watch the results come in? I might have a bottle of gin somewhere," she said with a mischievous look in her eye.

The open plan office was empty and dark apart from a single monitor bleeding a pale bluish white light onto Capello's face. He was looking at his pension, cashing in his insurance, collecting his retirement benefit. He swept a hand over his polished bald head, rubbed an eye with the knuckle of his right forefinger and yawned. It was exactly 2.57am and he had precisely three minutes before the new shift took over. After spending all these years in the business he had precious little to show for it. Now it was time. The plugged in flash drive lit up transferring the data, gigabytes of the stuff, high clearance pass-codes, usernames, operation manuals and most valuable of all a network map of all the servers and agents. It was an opportune time when everyone's attention would be on the result of the Scottish referendum.

A twinge of pain broke his concentration. He touched his jaw wincing. It was possibly an abscess and certainly not something that was going to go away any time soon. He hated dentists avoiding them whenever possible. Pain was nothing new to him but neither was his fear of dentists. The transfer of files seemed slow. He looked out the window across to the far side of the doughnut shaped building and saw a small pinprick of light on the third floor. The angry reddish scar on his neck seemed to tighten. An alert pinged indicating the transfer was complete. He pulled out the flash drive and put it in his pocket then began covering his tracks. He checked to see which PC was being used on the other side of the building. It was in the data analysis department, perfect.

He scrubbed clean his activity terminating the routes to his computer and redirected them to the night shift worker on the third floor, fortune was smiling on him. The monitor, the only source of light powered down leaving him in relative darkness. He checked his luminous watch, there was fifty seconds left. He hurried to the stairwell and climbed the stairs two at a time until he reached a door onto the flat roof. The air was cold and still. The first frost of the year glistened under a clear starlit sky. He looked over at the Cheltenham skyline, turned and made his way across the roof. Hidden behind a vent was an O-ring sealed case. He opened it and took out a small drone and controller loaded the drive onto it and sent it flying towards an open pick-up in the car park. Switching it off he packed up the controller and hid the box. Now he was clean if stopped on the way out.

2

Iona washed her hands in the faux marble basin in the lavatory and looked at herself in the mirror. She was tired. Her natural blonde hair in a bob, cut with an exaggerated fringe almost hiding one eye created an asymmetry that belied the natural balance of her face. Piercing clear blue eyes with an almost undetectable application of make-up and her only nod to jewellery was a pierced diamond stud above her right nostril. Someone once said when you're looking in the mirror that's not who you are. But she knew exactly what she was. Satisfied she took her LV handbag and went back to her desk. The flickering TV monitor confirmed what she had been hoping for. She put her head down on her crossed arms on the desk and looked up carefully at the figures. They were not all in yet but there was no doubting the result. It was YES. Despite all the odds it had happened. Iona's face flushed and a tear surprised her. She was not the emotional type usually but her feelings welled up inside as if it had been repressed all these years. There was mostly relief but also joy, apprehension and euphoria. She always thought it would happen but thinking and happening are two entirely different things. She had even prepared for it but in fear of disappointment, pushed the possibility away nudging it to the back of her mind, just in case it didn't happen. She carefully took out her contact lenses dabbing her cheeks with a paper handkerchief and put on a pair of rimless glasses. She was thinking how ridiculous it was to be on her own on such a momentous occasion as this and turned up the sound of the monitor on her desk.

"Scotland has spoken and the word is YES. I'm witnessing every emotion it's possible to express. There are tears, tears of joy as the enormity of this historic decision begins to sink in. There are tears being shed of despair from those opposed to independence and frankly here in George Square it's only the badges they wear that can tell some of them apart. There are also people wandering about in a daze totally stunned at the outcome. There are fireworks, bagpipes and cheering. Something really quite extraordinary has happened tonight and for the Scottish nation things will never be the same again. Scotland is now a sovereign country free of Westminster rule and the raw emotions openly on display here in George Square are indescribable. In all my years working for news on this channel I have never experienced anything anywhere near this and I've been trying to think of historical comparisons but with great difficulty. In the 1960's many countries gained independence from Britain, Kenya, Zambia, Uganda, Tanzania and many, many more before and after and this is what it must have been like in each and every one of them. The atmosphere is unbelievable. Let me see if I can get a few words here. Excuse me sir how do you feel about the decision and how will it affect you?"

"I'm numb. It's a bit scary, scary in an exciting way. I never thought we could do it and now we are independent. I don't know where my family is, I've been separated from them they're in the crowd somewhere. I can't wait to see their faces. This is life changing. This is the emergence of an old culture taking charge of its own destiny as a new country, absolutely fantastic. I'm sorry I have to find my family."

"Thank you, let's move on. Most of the No campaigners have melted away with the news but there are some left here at the steps of the George Watt Monument. Excuse me sir."

"It's a disaster, I'm gutted you'll not recognise the country in a year or two. If I was younger I would emigrate."

"Thank you. Well the party is beginning to get into full swing by the sounds of it and it may be a few days before it's over. This is Bill Duncannon live in George Square Glasgow now back to the studio."

Iona was tired and elated as the adrenalin began to wear off. She emailed her resignation letter to her department head Jane Caddish powered down the computer and opened her desk drawer emptying the contents into her rucksack. Having covered her assigned duties early she decided to cut short her night-shift stint and end her employment there and then with the firm. She always preferred working at night, with no one about there were fewer distractions. She looked around the open plan rows of empty desks and darkened monitors. The firm had been good to her and she had been good for it but now it was time to move on, no farewells no goodbyes, she hated goodbyes and now she was free just like Scotland. She took off her glasses and cleaned them. There was a red-eye flight from Heathrow getting into Edinburgh early there would be no problem catching it without a booking. She picked up her phone and began texting.

'Yippee *freedom for Scotland and me. Handed in my notice. Meet me at the airport don't forget my bag. X'*

"Are the results all in?"

"More or less."

"What's it looking like?"

"An emphatic yes."

"How emphatic?"

"Excluding spoilt papers 61% to 39."

Prime Minister Charles Keating muttered an oath under his breath. It had been difficult years since exiting Europe. Politically the Europeans were an easy scapegoat for the downturn in manufacturing and a massive balance of payments deficit with high unemployment and even higher taxes. VAT was now at 30%. He wasn't really surprised at the Yes vote despite everything he had thrown at the separatists, more threats he knew to be hollow, more promises he knew to be fake but the Scottish people had heard it all before and were immune. He still had one last card to play. The years had taken its toll. He had noticed greying at the temples and sallowness to the cheeks. An external sign of the daily infighting and backbiting, treachery and intrigue that was much more than the rough and tumble of an unpopular PM. Inside there was anxiety and confusion, sleepless nights and arguments with his wife. Fortunately only his closest friends and advisors had noticed the change. Coming from a wealthy family he didn't need the job but it was never about money it was all about power and the history books. He knew he would go down as the only Prime Minister to have been in a government that lost two unions. Now that his party was in disarray he needed a distraction away from his unpopular policies to unite his party. Scotland would be his Falklands that would pull them into line. He could not let Scotland go.

"There's no legality to this referendum Patrick none whatsoever. If the Government of Scotland act on this vote it will be a unilateral declaration of independence. I'll make sure it will not be recognised by the UN, NATO, the European Union or anybody else so they can go to hell. I will not preside over the breakup of Britain under any circumstances. A threat to the union is a threat to our existence and we must call on all of our resources to nip this nonsense in the bud."

Cabinet Secretary Sir Patrick Morris looked weary. It had been a long night and dawn was seemingly no nearer. He had served seven Prime Ministers but he had never witnessed the terminal decline of any government such as this one. He examined the papers on the table in front of him even though there was little to examine in an attempt to collect his thoughts. He peered over the top of his glasses at the PM.

"I don't think there's any doubt that they will act on this," he said. "They'll claim they have a democratic mandate. There are countries that Scotland has very close links with that will be sympathetic like Ireland, Iceland possibly Malawi, maybe one or two of the Nordic countries Norway or Denmark and then there's Canada, New Zealand..."

"Ok."

"...And then there are the meddling countries who would want to make things difficult for us like Russia, who knows maybe even China. They'll be queuing up to muddy the waters."

"Send a note to Arthur Douglas SIS. I want a team activated in Scotland for an operation right away; better start the ball rolling sooner rather than later. Call a COBRA meeting in an hour I want GCHQ, SIS, MI5 and the relevant depart heads and the Chief of the Defence Staff. Make sure that every single member that attends or knows about this meeting is vetted for any connection whatsoever to Scotland."

"Sir, your grandmother was Scottish."

3

The flight from Gatwick to Edinburgh was delayed by three hours and full. It was only pleading for the spare jump seats with check in staff that they managed to catch it at all. Iona McCallum and her partner Bjørge Tennfjord sat facing what could only be described as a wild good humoured raucous full-on party. It was much to the credit of the cabin crew who occasionally joined in, to allow the understandably high spirits on board. They did however draw the line at a travelling conga along the single aisle separating the rows.

"Are you going home?" asked a stocky red-faced man with a long grey beard wearing a kilt. He leaned forward expertly balancing a whisky in a plastic cup with one hand and in the other two open miniatures waiting to be poured.

Bjørge smiled. "No I'm from Norway."

"Near enough," he said taking a sip. "If you think about the country's name, the United Kingdom of Great Britain and Northern Ireland, what kind of name is that? We're still in the days of the empire. But if you examine the wording carefully, Britain appears to be England, Wales, Scotland. Northern Ireland is an add on. All these people trying to make us feel like Brits. Britain is just a collective noun for four countries, well three now. You're too young to remember when the Callaghan Government rigged the referendum in 1979 for devolution so that we couldn't possibly win. It required 40% of eligible voters to have voted but the register was so out of date, the figure couldn't be met, shocking. Is this your lassie?" Bjørge nodded.

He finished his drink and poured both miniatures into the cup put it down and stuck out his hand.

"Getting out of Europe was a huge mistake but every cloud has a silver lining and now we've got ours. The EU was like any relationship. There are things you don't like and no doubt things about you that are disliked by the other party, heaven knows no relationship is perfect but that's not the point it's a balancing act. The overall benefit to both parties should outweigh the negatives. Would anyone else like to take over the soapbox? My names Hector by the way."

"Bjørge and this is my girlfriend Iona." They shook hands.

"Iona, what a wonderful name it's my favourite girl's name. You know this is going to make a huge difference in Scotland and all this carry on about money. They should take my advice. I wrote to Cassie you know, never got a reply. Declare the currency a Scottish pound and peg it to the Euro. Has it ever struck you as being strange that abroad it's described as a Great British pound, try and find the Bank of Britain it doesn't exist. What they're really saying is England is Britain, scandalous. Now my brother flew to Johannesburg and he only had Scottish notes. The stewardess didn't want to take them until he pointed out that the airline was UK Air not English Air. He got his duty frees. It might seem petty but if we're allowed to print money we should be allowed to spend it. England missed a trick during the Euro referendum. They should have threatened to leave the UK union if Scotland kept England in Europe against its will. Would you like a drink? I've got more of these somewhere, the lassies on the flight are very generous."

"Maybe they're in your sporran Hector," said Iona.

"You're cheeky I like that. You'd be surprised at what I keep in my sporran," he said with a wink. "Maybe you wouldn't. No I just keep money oh and the phone of course. Can't go anywhere without it. Always gives me a bit of a surprise when it rings, know what I mean?" he said laughing. "Missed the vote myself, got stuck in Baku you know? Azerbaijan? I'm in the oil business. Their output isn't big but they wanted a consultant for a couple of weeks. Interesting place though have you ever been?" They shook their heads. "So what is it you do darling?"

"I'm a...was, a civil servant. I decided to go home and work for the Scottish government if they'll have me."

"No dear you're not going home you're coming home," he wrinkled his nose. "I'm sorry but I haven't got much time for civil servants nothing personal. What about you? Bjørge isn't it?"

Bjørge laughed. "I'm a civil servant too of sorts I work in the Norwegian embassy."

"Oh," Hector tapped his nose, "a spy. I've met plenty of spies. They follow you around pretending to be fixers for you but they're reporting everything you do back to HQ. Nice fellows most of them. I once complained that they never sent any female fixer spies, in the interest of gender equality you understand. They just thought I was a randy old devil. No faith. In some places I can't wear the kilt you know. Women are terrible they're forever trying to find out if you're wearing anything under it, sadly it's usually ugly middle-aged crones. I just tell them to keep their hands to themselves. They've no idea what I'm saying of course. Ah women, wonderful creatures. They're just like cars...the faster they are the more expensive they become, bless' em. I was once arrested in Bujumbura..."

"Ladies and gentlemen please fasten your seatbelts and ensure that your seat backs are in an upright position."

The television news presenter was taken slightly off guard. "Welcome back. We've been told that the First Minister of Scotland will be making a live appearance in about two hours. There has as yet been no statement from the Prime Minister so let's get reaction from abroad. Predictably the head of the Catalonian independence movement are first off the blocks congratulating the Scottish Government. In a statement just released they say the Basque people have a great affinity for Scotland and the Celtic people and offer their heartfelt congratulations. The Prime Minister of Finland has said that Scotland has democratically decided on its future and that decision should be respected. The Prime Minister of Poland has sent his congratulations, there are of course a large number of Poles living and working in Scotland. We'll be bringing more of those stories as they come in. Now, in the studio we have with us the business correspondent of the Financial Times Josephine Wellsby, Josephine what are the markets going to make of this and how will it affect the pound?"

"Well now that Scotland is an independent sovereign nation, all of the pre-referendum rhetoric will be forgotten and pragmatism will be the order of the day. While this is a seismic political event which will take a long time for the aftershocks to die down and let's face it a lot of horse trading will start between the two governments, I don't see a huge difference in the way the corporate community will approach business. It won't quite be business as usual but as close as it can be under these new circumstances. The markets are less concerned about politics and more about stability, financial forecasts and balance sheets and there is nothing to suggest that there is going to be a run on the banks or massive selling on the stock markets or a slide in the value of the pound after all

Scotland has been and always will be wedded to the rest of the UK's business models. They are still trying to come to terms and much more preoccupied with the effects of Britain having voted to leave Europe and its unforeseen consequences."

"Just in from Reuters is an unconfirmed report of a new credit rating issued by Standard and Poor for Scotland to be set at triple A."

"I'm not surprised that will make borrowing a lot cheaper for the new Scottish Government and it underlines what I think will happen when the markets open. However everything is in the melting pot until there is clarification from both governments."

"Also in our London studio patiently waiting and I thank you for that is Alan Scobie chief economist from the Economy UK website. Alan you've heard what Josephine was saying, are there any economic potholes on the road to Scottish fiscal sovereignty?"

"Potholes, certainly but the trouble with potholes is that when they fill with water you don't know how deep they are. Similarly there will be some fairly severe challenges that faces Scotland as it does with every country but I think the Scottish economy at present is diverse and robust enough to mitigate any threatening potholes. However the elephant in the room is the British Treasury. There will be a lot of very sore losers not just in the political establishment but also in the civil service especially very powerful departments like the Treasury. Don't forget, no matter what has been said before about Scots with their begging bowls, the rest of the UK will lose and they will not be at all happy about that. For example Scotland could invest heavily in wind and tidal renewables in a big way exporting surplus power to England and when, not if, oil prices reclaim the same dizzy heights, that would be the cherry on the icing on the cake. But I can honestly see the UK establishment desperately looking for ways to reign in a rampant Scottish economy."

"Josephine was talking about our exit from Europe, how important was that to the result and what do you think will happen next?"

"I think that was the tipping point because the majority in Scotland didn't want to leave Europe in the first place so there will be many Brussels meetings to determine where Scotland stands and frankly I think it's a no-brainer. Scotland will assume England's' place in Europe and if that happens business may take flight from the rest of the UK to Scotland, keen not to have trading barriers and that's another very big reason for Westminster to be particularly anxious at this time. I'm sure any future Scottish government will be only too pleased to welcome these businesses. However while the European exit set the referendum in motion I'm certain that the polls forecasting another Conservative Government next May was the decisive factor."

"Thank you Allan Scobie from Economy UK and Josephine Wellsby from the Financial Times. One interesting effect from today's result is that there has been an avalanche of applications from England and Wales for Scottish passports. Of course if Scotland retains membership of Europe and with the rest of the UK out that means those holders of Scottish passports could live and work and have all the benefits that existed before the UK left. In the scenario of a Scotland as part of the EU does that mean there will be customs and immigration posts between the two countries? David McFarlane joins us now from Coldstream right on the Scottish borders, David."

"Yes Alison, I've been talking to people here about just that and there have been mixed views. Businesses that operate in both countries are alarmed at the prospect of passports and immigration checks here, they feel it will hamper their trade. A lot of people living on the other side of the River Tweed depend on the services and infrastructure of Coldstream. I asked some of the locals earlier and this is what they had to say."

"I'm a pensioner and I have to cross the bridge at least once a week to the Post Office to get my pension and do some shopping, I am worried I don't know what's going to happen."

"Well I actually live in Northumberland and I think all this is great, I've been thinking of moving to Scotland for a while anyway and this has made my mind up. So I'm really here looking at the property market."

"I've been a postmistress here for nearly forty years and there are a lot of worried people especially from the other side of the river. I would hope the Scottish and English governments are going to have some kind of relaxed understanding about the border between the two countries otherwise there's going to be mayhem."

"Mayhem in Coldstream Janet?"

Cars were blowing their horns as they passed Bute House, home of the First Minister and fireworks lit the dawn sky. Janet Cassie looked down at the scene from the window of her apartment as her husband switched off the television and put his feet up on a stool. Her mobile phone texting note was almost continuous. The room had decanted campaign managers, cabinet ministers, friends and relatives who had gone leaving the First Minister and her husband alone at last.

"There'll be no mayhem in Coldstream or anywhere else caused by this office. There's no need for border posts between Scotland and England. I can't speak for Westminster though they might want to build another Hadrian's Wall for all I know."

"I'm very proud of you. You realize you are going to be Scotland's very first Prime Minister?"

"Until we have a Scottish general election, do you like the sound of that? I actually don't care who Scotland's Prime Minister is the really important thing is that we did it, we finally did it. There are people on the street dancing and partying. There's a line doing the Conga. I can't believe it I really can't I'm going to get all emotional when I deliver my speech in the morning. I've had hundreds of texts I can't keep up with them and all the emails."

"Would you like a drink now?"

"No and neither are you I want you standing next to me when I give this speech and I don't want you looking bleary eyed."

"Have you heard anything from London?"

"You mean the PM? Not a cheep."

"Be careful of him Janet somehow I can't see him just taking this on the chin."

Janet Cassie sat down at her desk in the corner and looked at the speech on her computer.

"You know the strategy unit write great speeches but sometimes they're sterile and need personalizing. I'm not joking sometimes when I'm reading them I start yawning. It could be that they knowingly leave in things for me to change. But I think this is about right, do you want to hear it." John Cassie was fast asleep.

"What I'm going to say now must never be repeated outside of this room. I want an excuse to send in the troops. I need disorder, riots, agent provocateurs responding to unionist protests and fighting with the police. The object of the exercise is to impose martial law and suspend the Scottish parliament. Now how do we go about that?"

Tired faces of selected cabinet ministers summoned to Cabinet Office Briefing Room A (COBRA) looked at the PM. Some had an inkling before they came what the meeting was for but most were taken aback by the PM's tone. Sir Cyrus Steele, SIS, Arthur Douglas Director of MI5 and Sir Brian Mowbray Director of GCHQ weren't at all surprised and had already prepared for it.

"Prime Minister Since the very beginning of the 2014 Scottish Referendum, GCHQ have been monitoring all digital traffic including emails, video chatter, texts and phone calls with GPS and Cell-net mast triangulation of all members of the SNP's MSP's, MP's and MEP's. Using a suite of sophisticated algorithms we have collated data that after analysis shows a very small proportion of the membership has any kind of radical views. A forecast suggests that statistically the percentage is actually smaller than other UK political parties. Independence social media traffic has long since shifted from abusive name calling to satire and mockery, a much more effective way of damaging an opponent and the main stream media cannot satirise satire or mock mockery. Within the department it has been challenging to say the least for covert monitoring because of the large number of Scots working at GCHQ. This has reduced our flexibility. There is also an increasing number of Scottish staff considering resigning and work for the Scottish Government."

"Thanks for that Brian, Arthur?"

"These are extraordinary times Prime Minister and while I recognise that a threat to the Union is a threat to the country we could be embarking on another war similar to that which happened in Ireland. Added to that our foreign agents have been monitoring diplomatic traffic and finding that there could be consequences if we intervene. There could even be consequences from some of our allies abroad."

"What consequences?"

"It would be sanctions of one sort or another depending on what happened."

"Stuff them it's none of their business. Cyrus I want you to organise unionist groups to demonstrate and I also want you to set up rival groups purporting to be separatists to disrupt the demonstrations, tyre burning, stone throwing that kind of thing. This has to be seen to be an entirely Scottish issue though and nothing to do with us. Use the kind of tactics that would be deployed on foreign soil to destabilize a government. I want a targeted explosion with limited collateral damage, I don't want to know the details I need plausible deniability but I'm not giving you carte blanche."

Line after line of cars slowed down on the Forth Road Bridge and stopped and remarkably not one single horn was heard as the commuters listened to the First Minister addressing the Scottish Parliament on their radios.

"Freedom is a much used and abused word in the English language but I have never known the use of the word freedom to taste this sweet. The people of Scotland were asked a very simple question, do you want an independent Scotland and the answer was a resounding yes. Scotland will be a sovereign independent country. My heart is bursting with pride for all of you who were brave enough, strong enough and believed enough in an independent Scotland and now the dream is a reality. They said we were too wee, too poor and too stupid to run our own affairs well now we can show them how wrong they were. Of course we will still have very close ties with our neighbours only this time it will be as equals. We will be making decisions in Scotland for Scotland that will benefit the Scottish people. No longer will we sit on the side-lines while decisions are made hundreds of miles away. We are free from a Government we didn't vote for who pursued an ideology we didn't want. I will give you a solemn promise, Scotland will be a better place for all the people, not just Scots and not just a privileged few."

Iona and Bjørge anxiously watched the carousel as it stopped with the last of the bags. Most of the passengers had left baggage reclaim and the rest were soon gone leaving them alone.

"That's very annoying, we'll have to find someone to report them missing." Said Bjørge.

"Excuse me were you the last ones to board the flight?" It was a baggage handler wearing a day-glow high viz yellow jacket and ear defenders around his neck. Bjørge nodded. "It was too late for your bags to go in the hold."

He held open the door for one of the cabin staff who was pushing a trolley into the arrivals hall carrying Iona's pink hard shell and Bjørge's large bright blue rucksack. They said their thanks and left the arrivals hall.

"I'm dying to get to bed," she said. Pushing the trolley through the open automatic doors they stopped to see if there was a cab.

4

In the early hours the Secretary of State for Scotland, Gordon Hamilton's staff car negotiated through the London traffic. He was the consummate professional politician who had survived many brickbats from his opponents and sometimes even from those he would have considered colleagues. His job was on the line now and he had made it clear to the PM that he wanted to keep it. His vanity and lack of humility was legend amongst the civil service. He was once heard saying to a junior minister at the Strangers Bar, "It's hard to be humble when you have nothing to be humble about." His car stopped and the chauffeur opened the door. He made his way through the Ionic columns guarding the entrance to Dover House in Whitehall, London's Scotland Office and went straight into a meeting with his advisors and senior staff.

"I've had a call from the PM," he said taking his seat at the head of the table. "For the present the Scotland Office will continue here in Dover House. All essential personnel, electronic equipment and files have already been removed from Melville House in Scotland and relocated here. Our new role will be to analyse data emerging from Scotland and prepare reports for number ten."

Lord Killburn the Parliamentary Under Secretary of State for Scotland looked puzzled.

"Who is supplying the data and how will we know it's accurate?"

"Heather do you know if all the vetting procedures have been carried out on staff?"

"Most of them," she said looking at her notes, "of those here only PR are still waiting for clearance."

"David and Lindsay, I'm terribly sorry but could you possible leave us there's some updated security clearances that have not run their course yet, it's a temporary blip," he said as they got up and left.

"Now I believe the information will be coming from GCHQ so it will not reach us until it has been verified. As you know there is no legal basis for a declaration of independence and so there will not be an automatic handing over of power. The position of her Majesty's Government is that Scotland is very much still part of the UK and will continue to be so and we must do all in our power to ensure that Scotland remains in the UK. Now I know that there are many people in Scotland who are deeply unhappy with the result of the referendum and my fear is that over time they will express their views perhaps forcibly. So it is up to us to convince the Scottish Government and the people of Scotland that the only future that exists is within the UK. It has been given a code name..."

There was a tap at the door and an aide appeared. "Excuse me sir the Prime Minister is giving a statement live on television." Hamilton nodded and the aide switched it on.

"...and the Scottish government have ignored warnings that the referendum has no basis in law. Therefore there will be a number of measures that I will detail in the House in due course to ensure that Scotland does not simply enter into the wilderness. I have a duty of care and responsibility to all citizens of the United Kingdom and I will not fail in that duty. These are extremely difficult and uncertain times but we will prevail. This government will not abandon the people of Scotland for an ideology of separation."

"I suspect we've just heard the starting pistol for Operation False Dawn," said Hamilton drily.

"Breaking news. There are reports coming in of a massive explosion at the Scotland Office in Edinburgh. So far there are no casualty figures but the blast has caused extensive structural damage to the building. Melville House is a late 17th Century category A listed building. Police Scotland has cordoned off the area. No group has claimed responsibility but speculation is growing that this is a marker thrown down by a dissident separatist group reacting to the Prime Ministers speech in the House of Commons. The Scottish Government has condemned any use of violence and is appealing for calm. Our reporter David McFarlane heard the blast and he is live in Melville Crescent. David what's the latest?"

"Actually I live not very far from the Scotland Office and the explosion woke me up at exactly 6.32am. It was a single explosion that rattled my windows, now I'm told by the police that there was a five minute warning just long enough to get the security and cleaning staff clear of the building.

About thirty cars parked nearby were damaged and windows were blown out of neighbouring offices..."

"...We're just showing some footage from our video drone David and it's looking like the building has been so badly damaged it may have to be demolished, is there any information where the blast originated?"

"Without confirmation what I've heard is that the explosion came from a parked vehicle outside the building probably a lorry. It appears from the wreckage of the vehicle that a wall of what looks like sand filled sacks were stacked inside, lining the furthest side of the lorry from the building. The effect of this would have been to maximize the blast towards the Scotland Office and minimize the damage to surrounding properties. Clearly this attack was not intended to kill anyone but it is significant that the target, Melville House, is one of the clearest symbols of the power of the Secretary of State for Scotland and therefore this could be seen as an attack on Westminster. I should add a word of caution about which group is responsible. Sources close to senior police officers have told me that they are puzzled by the pointlessness of this attack and that whoever planned and executed it had extensive knowledge about explosives so this may not be a haphazard group of people angry at what the Prime Minister said in the House of Commons. They knew exactly what they were doing. Actually if I could just catch his eye, Chief Superintendent George Grieve is just here. Chief Superintendent could we have a quick word, do you have an update on casualties?"

"There have been five people taken to hospital for minor injuries that are not life threatening, mostly from flying glass and roof slates. We will be giving a full statement shortly."

"Do you have any information as to the group responsible?"

"Not as yet, what we know is that this was a well-planned and co-ordinated attack by more than one person. We are monitoring CCTV cameras in the area."

Two saltires hung limply on poles at either side of the fireplace in the Cabinet meeting room at Bute House. The First minister sat with her back to the double windows at the head of the mahogany table. Behind her a circular regency mirror reflected an image of worried looking cabinet ministers, aides, PR and the newly appointed Police Scotland Chief Constable. Janet Cassie pulled her ladder back chair closer to the table and glanced up at him.

"This development is very worrying Paul, there's something very strange going on, have you had any Intel?"

"We have no idea who in Scotland would have the skills but it's also the speed that it happened is very odd. This was a well-planned professionally executed operation that was not a spur of the moment last minute exercise and I would think it was most likely carried out by a group with military training. I believe there are also bus loads of people coming to Glasgow and Edinburgh from Manchester, Birmingham and Liverpool to attend a demonstration opposing independence. So that could well be a flashpoint but we don't know how all this is being orchestrated."

"Is there going to be a counter demonstration?"

"There doesn't appear to be any signs so far that there will be and again you would have to ask the question what would be the point? I have to say Ma'am as far as intelligence is concerned we are being shut out of a real time feed of information that we rely on from the security and information gathering services at Cheltenham."

"I'm sorry I don't follow are you saying that SIS and GCHQ have stopped sharing information?"

"The Scottish Recording Centre (SRC) has received no information under the Milk-white arrangement since the Yes result. We have been effectively disconnected and what's more the funding to continue staffing SRC has stopped."

"I have been extremely concerned in the past about the SRC and its operations in Scotland. For example who does it report to apart from Police Scotland and to what extent were they involved in collecting data on the independence movement," said the First Minister.

"We have no evidence of SRC tracking politicians and Independence members but it's quite possible that there were two SRC's one inside the other reporting directly to GCHQ. You know what these organisations are like Ma'am, the left hand doesn't know what the right hand's doing and of course all Military Police are under direct control of London."

"We must have control over our own security services. Do we have contingency and what stage are we at in the process of setting up our own security and intelligence unit?"

"There are several commercial companies in Dundee and Leith that we are checking out for security and suitability. We could absorb them until a permanent security service is in operation."

"Paul, is Westminster responsible for this bomb?" There was a hushed tense silence.

"In the absence of any evidence to the contrary, that is a theory we cannot discount."

"They are looking for an excuse. We must ensure that our supporters don't get sucked into this. Graham what are the media saying?"

"It's what you'd expect, headlines like 'Scottish bombers blast Scotland Office' with a threat that Scotland is on the verge of anarchy and disorder. Another asks 'Are we witnessing the rise of the Scottish Republican Army?' That's from the broadsheets the tabloids are in a foaming frenzy. 'Mother of four escapes Scottish terror blast.' 'Scots warning blast to England' and so on. The thrust of the main stream media campaign seems to be to whip up fear resentment and hatred towards the Scottish Government. The social media trend is firmly towards a Westminster conspiracy theory. The Westminster Government has issued a statement holding the Scottish Government responsible for the security of all the people in Scotland."

"It seems to me that we have to avoid a confrontation at all costs with bussed in unionists. Graham start getting the message out. London are spoiling for a fight and we won't give it to them. Now a press release. The Scottish Government deplores this bombing and will not rest until those responsible are found. There is evidence that forces outside of Scotland may be responsible, we will stand firm against the bombers and we will never give in to violence."

"What evidence?"

"We don't have any if they want to play games so will we. Paul I want you to go ahead with these companies and in setting up our own security and intelligence unit. If we have any staff seconded to MI5, SIS or GCHQ get them back here quick. What about 5 Military Intelligence Battalion?"

"There is a bit of confusion about chain of command that needs to be sorted out so we're told."

"What about the armed services."

"An order has gone out for all personnel to be confined to barracks."

An aide came in. "Ma'am the American President is on the line."

"You've got a lovely soft voice my dear but my hearing isn't as good as it used to be."

RIE Emergency Department Junior Doctor Jāyah smiled. "You've had a bit of a shock Annabelle I was saying that we just wanted to keep an eye on you for a short while just to make sure all is OK."

"I shouldn't be here there's nothing wrong with me, just a few scratches, I feel like a phoney when I look around the ward."

"What were you doing out early in the morning anyway?"

"I always get up early and let Mimi out she's a Siamese. I stay with her for a little while in the garden she gets frightened by the traffic if she's alone. Are the others ok?"

"They'll be fine but they're a lot younger than you are. Oh I see your surname is McCallum. Your daughter isn't Iona by any chance?"

"Yes do you know her? She's my eldest daughter she must be worried about me."

"We went to St Andrews together, what a coincidence."

"She works for the government you know. I've no idea what she does. She was travelling up from London, should have arrived in Edinburgh by now. I have three daughters and they are so unlike each other. Funny the two youngest ones are very independent minded but they would have preferred to stay in Britain but Iona is like me, she wants a future where we make our own decisions. I'm not going to ask what you think, it wouldn't be fair. Such a pity about that lovely building, all that history it's so sad. I pass it every day you know, I hope they rebuild it."

"Hello Mum," Iona McCallum came in. "Dottie, hi I forgot you worked here. You look terrible Mum are you alright?"

"It's mostly superficial cuts and bruises and maybe a little shock," said Dr Jāyah we've checked her out and there's nothing broken or damaged. It's good to see you again Iona, I don't know where the time flies, look in by before you leave. We'll have to meet up for a chat."

"Of course thanks Dottie," the door closed.

"It's lovely to see you Iona what's happening in Scotland dear, I don't understand?"

"Are you strong enough to travel Mum?"

"I think so."

Iona took her mother's hand and looked at the cuts caused by the flying glass. "I want you to stay with Aunty Kath in Inverness for a while it's just in case things might get a bit rough here."

"I don't feel like travelling all the way to Inverness dear."

"Don't worry I'll hire a private ambulance, you can have a nice snooze on the way."

"What about you?"

"I travelled up with Bjørge, he's at the house. There's a lot of work for me to do in Scotland now that we are independent."

"How is Bjørge has he left his job too?"

"No he put in a transfer from the Embassy in Belgrave Square to the Consulate General in Rutland House."

"You know you've never actually told me what it is you do?"

"Oh I don't like talking about it Mum." There was an awkward silence. "I work, used to work in Cheltenham, analysing, prioritizing, trying to make sense of whatever passes across my desk and usually there are things going on I think I understand, but just now there are lots of things going on that I don't understand. We've decided to stay here. My country needs me. Sorry I'm not making any sense".

"I know you worked in Cheltenham but what's there?"

"CESG the Communications-Electronics Security Group it's the Information Security arm of GCHQ. Now, are you any the wiser?"

"Not really."

"Mum I know you don't like mobile phones but this is a special one keep it with you, it's very important. My mobile numbers on it, it's the only way I'm going to be able to keep in touch."

"What's special about it?"

"Nobody can listen in," she whispered.

5

"...This has been a day of extraordinary events. First the result of the referendum with Scotland firmly voting for independence and then the bombing of the Scotland Office. No one has yet claimed responsibility but speculation is mounting that it could be the work of unionists in response to the election result. That's a summary of the news for now and from me Alison Holt and now over to Helen Butler."

"Welcome to Holyrood Tonight the programme that seeks to make sense of tomorrow's political news stories today. I am Helen Butler and with me in the studio are the leaders of the four main opposition parties. But of course the big political story is Scotland's future. This has been a day that few thought they would ever live to see, a majority of people living and working in Scotland voting overwhelmingly for independence. While all the rhetoric that is being traded between Westminster and Holyrood is heating up the immediate question tonight is where does that leave the Scottish unionist parties who fought so hard to try to convince people to stay within the UK and failed? In the coming days, weeks and months Scotland will start the process of assuming full sovereignty on all matters so how will that change the political landscape of the country and the parties within? Ritchie McKenzie can I start with you, your former Scottish Labour party leader said she wouldn't recognise the result of a second referendum is that still party policy?"

"We're in a political no-man's land. None of us have been here before..."

"...Yes but are you going to respect the democratic wishes of the voters?"

"Well whether we respect the vote or not the legality of holding this referendum in the first place is very much in doubt and had it been 100% legal of course we would accept the outcome..."

"...So are you saying your party will not recognize the result of the referendum is that right?"

"Well the results are not long in and there needs to be a great deal of discussions some of which are on-going as we speak but it is difficult because we have not been here before."

"Crawford Black leader of the Scottish Conservative Party is also here in the studio. What is your view and that of the Scottish Conservatives about the result?"

"The Conservative party position has been clear from the outset..."

"...Are we talking about the Scottish Conservatives or the UK party?"

"Both, we are reading from the same hymn sheet. It is entirely proper to question the legality as the Labour party have done also because our society depends entirely in upholding the law and so while I understand that there is a democratic consensus in Scotland for more powers it has to be done in an unambiguous manner with regard to legality. Next thing will be the Isle of Wight holding a referendum. It reminds me of the Ealing comedy a Passport to Pimlico. We all have to abide by the rule of law and this result is clearly illegal."

"There are a number of countries who are prepared to recognize the vote, what is your view on that?"

"Well of course those that say these things have their own reasons for pursuing that point of view and really they ought to mind their own business."

"And now in our Edinburgh studio is Janet Cassie First minister and leader of the SNP. First Minister the referendum vote is illegal so nothing has changed. Isn't this putting Scotland on a collision course with Westminster?"

"The decision not to allow a second referendum by the Conservative Westminster Government was political not a legal one and it was taken by a government that has only one MP in Scotland..."

"...Have you noticed that if you listen to politicians long enough their clichés become familiar?" said Bjørge exasperated.

"Do you think we'll get a straight answer from any of them?" Iona McCallum sat on a mushroom coloured sofa with her feet resting on the coffee table in her mother's comfortable living room with her partner, watching the interview.

"There's a lot to be said for things left unsaid."

"That's deep," she said

"I don't know what all the fuss is about. The political ideology of both Scotland and England has polarized so much and the paths that both countries have chosen are so different that a break was always going to be inevitable. Can you imagine if there had been a United Kingdom of Scandinavia led by King Carl XVI Gustaf of Sweden?" he asked.

"Yes," said Iona mischievously opening a bag of crisps.

"It was a rhetorical question. There would be chaos absolute chaos."

When they argued which wasn't very often, he would make a firm stand on the subject leaving an empty silence, a silence that she knew he didn't like and then as always he capitulated. Strangely, he seemed oblivious that it was just a game of sorts. Only she was aware of the rules.

"What do you think is going to happen next?" he asked.

"I had a very bad feeling about it, that's why I decided to leave Cheltenham. I have a few contacts in the business who know I'm here. I'm going to be needed because I think there could be an attempt to destabilize and undermine the government. Mum will be a lot safer in Inverness."

"How bad do you think it'll get?"

"Worse-case scenario? Civil war or maybe a long smouldering guerrilla campaign or maybe London will see the wisdom of just having a new and truly equal partner."

"I think you're wrong about a civil war. Somebody in Westminster must remember the mistakes made in Ireland and anyway what makes you so sure that there will be a campaign against the Scottish Government?"

Iona looked at him and sighed. "I can't tell you its top secret."

"Why don't we have a holiday in Stavanger mum and dad are always asking about you."

"My Norwegian isn't very good."

"Very funny they speak English better than you and me, come on you've packed in your job you're free." Bjørge helped himself to a crisp. "Yuk what flavour is that?"

"Beetroot Horseradish & Dill," Iona smiled and turned off the TV as her mobile rang out. "Hello?...yes Iona speaking..." There was a long pause as she listened intently then looked at Bjørge. "When?...I'll be there." She pressed the red phone on her mobile and smiled at him. "I've got a new job I can't take time off and neither can you if you're going to be transferred. Have you ever thought what it would be like being a dad?" she mused.

"No not really, why?"

"You'd better start thinking about it."

Bjørge stared in amazement. "Serious?" Iona nodded. He picked her up twirling her around spilling the crisps and let out a shout. "Fantastic," he laid her gently onto the sofa. "When did you, how, when will it...?"

"...I had an idea that I could be pregnant last week and took a couple of tests then I did a third which confirmed it. I'm going to make an appointment tomorrow to see the Doctor but it's got to be another seven months away at least. It's a boy."

"How do you know?"

"I just know and I've already chosen a name."

"Really, what is it?"

"Not telling."

"Don't I have a say?"

"No, I don't want some weird Norwegian boy's name, having Tennfjord as a surname is going to be bad enough." She said then mimicked him, "how about Eghart or Diedrich or Geirvald?"

"What's wrong with Eghart that's my father's name?"

"No it's not its Hartløv."

"Um...Hartløv Eghart Tennfjord."

Iona sniffed. "What are you doing?"

"Texting mum and dad."

"I'd rather you waited until after I see the Doctor. Maybe in a couple of weeks' time we'll go to Norway and tell your parents I really would like to meet them....What's this? I've just received an email from the office," she said sitting upright staring at her phone. "Listen to this;"

Iona you must return to GCHQ at once. Since you have the highest DV security clearance possible you are in possession of sensitive information that must not fall into the hands of foreign governments therefore it is imperative that you return immediately. In any case your contract expressly stipulates that you must work out a thirty day notice before leaving. I cannot impress on you enough how important it is for your department, your colleagues and for your own position that you return straight away. Failure to do so may imply that you are a category one security risk in which case a warrant may be issued for your arrest. We note that you are at the top of your pay scale and incentives are in place to substantially increase that on your return. Please consider very carefully your options.

Jane Caddish.'

"I can't believe she sent that email. So I either co-operate and get a pay rise or I get locked up," she said. "How dare they threaten me. It doesn't make any sense I never thought they would react like this...very strange. They've just made a big big mistake. This changes everything I can't stay here I'll have to move tonight. Make yourself at home they won't bother you, you're Norwegian not Scottish. You may get some visitors Just say you're house sitting, you know nothing. I was prepared to play the game by the rules but now the gloves are off."

"I have no idea what you're talking about."

"Good, keep it that way," she said giving him a kiss.

"Where will you go?"

"Oh I don't know. Actually I bumped into an old Uni friend at A & E I hadn't seen for a long time. She was treating mum. She lives in the New Town area and I might be able to crash out there. I'm going to have to do something with this phone and use my office backup, so GCHQ won't be able to track me on it. Now listen to me, no twitter no Facebook, no social media. There is a chat app called mirror+ and I know for a fact that their encryption hasn't been broken, we can communicate through that and if you want to send an email download the Black-watch email client, it uses the latest encryption. If you want to get the hell away from here and go to Stavanger I quite understand."

"And miss all the fun? I don't think so. Look is there anything I can do to help?"

"You're on their radar so they will be tracking you hoping to find me. So we can't meet."

Iona used a secure overwriting app to destroy files and folders, addresses and emails on her phone put it in a padded envelope she found in her mother's roll top desk, wrote an address on it and handed it to Bjørge.

"Post this for me first thing tomorrow morning."

"OK who's that to?"

"It's an ambiguous fictitious name and address in Aberdeen but Royal Mail will keep on attempting to find its proper destination which doesn't exist and it could take a long time. It'll keep them off the scent for a few days, continually moving until the extended battery dies."

"Do you need a gun, I have contacts?" he said raising his eyebrows.

Iona laughed. "Don't be silly Bjørge I'm just an intelligence & data analyst not Josephine Baker."

"Who?"

"The Black Pearl, the Créole Goddess, she was a singer and actress who helped the French resistance by smuggling out messages hidden in her sheet music. Are you sure you're not a spy for the Norwegian Government?"

"Curses my cover is blown, the Norwegian Government is very keen to know what your tastes in music, movies and crisps are. I'm a lowly cultural attaché. I organize meetings and events."

"Could be a cover."

"Ok when have I ever wanted to know about your boring work?"

Iona smiled as she sent a text then hurriedly packed a small rucksack with clothes etc. "Do you have any money? I can't use my credit or debit cards," she said.

"Fifty Quid. Are you not staying here tonight?"

"I can't stay here. When you get an email like that from Jane Caddish you take note. Fifty-quid's not enough let's go find a cash machine and a Tesco, I want to try Prosecco and Elderberry crisps."

"Is that wise?"

6

The lift stopped at the sixteenth floor and the door opened. Colin Reid emerged carrying a small rucksack over one shoulder followed by a blue cloud of smoke from the remains of a spliff, a mixture of cannabis and tobacco. He stopped, nipped off the end stamped on the glowing ember on the concrete floor and put what little was left in his pocket. The key turned in the door of flat 64 and he entered. The atmosphere inside was homely and not unpleasant but the air was stale and in need of an open window. He popped his head into the living room. His father Alec was asleep on the couch with the TV still on and the sound turned off. He heard his mother in the kitchen washing the lunchtime dishes. Doris always seemed to be working there. She stopped as he went in and looked up at him. In her late sixties, she hadn't bothered dying her grey hair and there was a frailty he hadn't noticed before.

"How did you get on at the dentist?" she asked.

"Fine. DWP have sanctioned me again, another six months without money. Back to the food bank, some people who come in think I work there. She didn't believe I had to go and get a tooth out. Just a young lassie. I showed her the blood, but she probably thought I'd been in a fight...anyway she's likely just making up her quota I suppose."

"Don't worry love, we'll manage."

Colin looked round the kitchen. The white fridge freezer was covered in magnets. A Native American chieftain, a large butterfly, an I heart Scotland pen, a pair of Scottie dogs one black the other white. It was all depressingly kitsch and cute. A cupboard door had been left open revealing a few half empty packets of gravy salt, macaroni and herbs. The worktops were untidy and a drawer was half open with something sticking out. It was all symptomatic of depression and futility.

"What's for tea?"

"I'm afraid it's just corn beef and tatties luv, is that ok?"

"Sounds good to me. Are you all right Ma?"

"Of course I am, don't worry about me you've got your own problems. Things will change now Scotland is independent, you'll see."

"I hope so Ma it can't get any worse."

"Are you still taking your medicine?" she asked nervously.

Colin had been in the army for just over five years. He had done tours in Afghanistan and Iraq. Suffering from PTSD, he had been discharged after a brawl in a local pub that had left five people hospitalized. The pushers and dealers on the estate had left him and his parents alone frightened of his army training and unpredictable outbursts.

"Of course and it's helping a lot. I'm thinking of moving in with Jenny."

"In Perth?"

"Yes. This is a terrible place, can the council not find you anything better?"

"No we're too old, the young ones have priority."

"The best thing about this flat is the view of Hampden Park and Celtic Park even then you can't see the pitches."

Doris smiled. "We had a lot of friends here but they've all gone."

"I get angry Mum."

"I know."

"No I don't mean that. I get angry when I see what the fat cats get away with and the poor people are left picking up the bill. They'll be alright as long as money talks and the poor don't listen. Do you know what quantitative casing is? It's not even a proper phrase. It's made up to hide the fact that crooked greedy banks are getting billions of newly printed money from their pals in the Government. Sometime I feel like reclaiming that money, robbing a bank, I could get some army mates, it's our money after all."

Doris had heard all this before. "Are you hungry?"

"Getting that way Ma," he smiled. "Me rob a bank, do you think I'd get away with it? Piggy bank maybe," he shook his head.

George Square was quiet until an orange streak crossing the night sky in an arc landed on a police patrol car and burst into flames. Two policemen staggered out of the vehicle on fire and rolled on the ground to put the flames out. More Molotov cocktails flew towards the retreating unprotected police who were caught off guard. A small group of Nationalists who were watching got caught up in the barrage. An explosion was heard and some gunfire. Sirens mingling with car alarms echoed along the street as vans started to arrive carrying riot police and armed response units. More firebombs exploded against the transparent high-impact polycarbonate shields. The police responded with tear gas. Several tyres were lit causing acrid smoke to drift towards the police lines. A choking fog that enveloped everyone created confusion and alarm from the passing public caught up in the demonstration. Ambulances started to arrive amid a shower of bricks. A cameraman live linked to a satellite van broadcasting around the world fell to the ground struck by a missile. An order was issued from an officer to use baton rounds to disperse the crowd while snatch squads tried to get the ring leaders. A car was set on fire and shortly after came the sound of a shop window being smashed. The chaos was faithfully relayed through satellite to hundreds of millions of television viewers worldwide. Television reporters attempted pieces-to-camera and interviews amid the pandemonium adding to the drama.

"I saw two policemen with charred clothing being taken off by ambulance. It is very difficult to speak because the air is full of smoke from the burning tyres and the tear gas that has drifted our way. I can see a number of Union Jacks waving at the far end of the street which is the direction the missiles are coming from and I haven't seen a single Saltire. I haven't been able to talk to anyone understandably this is an emergency but it's looking like the police are readying themselves to move forward to try and disperse the crowd."

The police charged the protesters who turned and ran melting into side streets. Three police helicopters and two news helicopters hovered high above with search lights strafing the scene below.

"It's hard to imagine this kind of scene ever happening on mainland Britain but now we don't have to it's happening right now. Chief Inspector what is the situation at the moment?"

"Now that the crowds are dispersing our helicopters using specialized equipment will be tracking them. The Fire Brigade can now get to the burning tyres and put them out."

"Thank you and now back to the studio."

Colin ended up where he always did when things were going against him, at the Well. It was a pub not far from George Square along a narrow lane.

You might find it by accident but that was unlikely. He went there for three reasons. The owner was Dougie an old school mate who Colin had helped out in the past when a partner tried to run off with the profits. Colin tracked him down and 'persuaded' him to return the money and as a consequence Dougie knowing Colin's financial circumstances was always grateful. That hospitality was never abused. Secondly Colin needed a drink and there was always a good selection of real ales on tap. And then there was the clientele the flotsam of Glasgow's best and most colourful would float in and out like the tide always leaving behind interesting sometimes funny memories. Tonight it was quiet. The younger customer numbers had dropped a little since Dougie got rid of the one-arm-bandit. He always hated the things. Poor people putting the last of the housekeeping money into the machine then shambling up to the bar wanting a tab. Dougie was pouring Colin a pint of Happy Chappie.

"What's going on out there Coll sounds like a riot," he waited for the froth to subside.

"I don't know, I don't get involved in all that politics stuff."

Colin looked along the bar. There were four young guys two of them Asian. They looked like students sharing a laugh and a joke. Colin noticed they were wearing saltire badges.

"Did you hear about Gregor?" Dougie put the pint on the bar and wiped his hands on a cloth.

Colin hesitated over the drink. "No?"

"He was giving his old lady a smacking when the police arrived. So the wife and three polis are in hospital and he's in the nick no doubt getting what for."

Gregor was one of Colin's pals. They had enlisted together. Colin shook his head and sipped the beer. "That's three guys from my regiment that I know of ending up in the clink."

"Oh-oh look out," said Dougie. Five burly guys with shaved heads carrying a furled Union Jack came in.

"It's all happening oot there what a rammy. Five pints of your best barkeep," said the one holding the flag. "What have we got here, filthy separatists?"

"I don't want any trouble in here guys, on your way."

"Who asked your opinion? Is this a separatist's pub?"

"Ok that's it, out or I'll call the police"

They laughed. "The Polis are far too busy on the Square. Hey guys if you don't take these badges aff I'll rip them aff."

"Give us a break we're just in for a drink," one said.

"Gie ye a break, al gie ye a break awright."

Colin looked at Dougie, stepped down from the stool and moved away from the bar slightly tapping the flag man on the shoulder. He turned as two others moved round nearer Colin. The students sensing an opportunity to escape bolted for the door.

"Are you a separatist as weel?"

"I'm English but if it puts me on the opposite side from you I could be tempted."

"Look guys you've had your fun you've scared the Nat's' off now on your way ok?" asked Dougie.

"I'm talking to your pal here."

"Dougie can you put this safe?" He said sliding his pint across the bar and at the same time swung his arm round and caught the flag man on the throat. His foot connected with his friend's knee and they both fell on the floor in agony. "What's it to be lads?" he said calmly with his hands out palms facing upwards. They picked up their injured friends and left. Three old crones at the far end of the bar who had been enjoying the cabaret cackled, clapped and hooted their approval.

7

Iona's bus travelled along a wet and windy Princes Street towards Leith. She had never learned to drive because she didn't need to having lived in cities all her life. She wiped the condensation from the window and gazed out at the iconic Edinburgh Castle. It was a view she never got tired of though she had seen it hundreds of times before. The changing light and weather always made it look different somehow. Lines of raindrops dribbled down the window and a wave of depression took hold. She tried to analyse her mood and couldn't. Maybe it was a hormonal change or maybe it was just the effects of a wet Edinburgh morning. Her text tone purred like a cat and she quickly retrieved it from her bag hoping nobody had heard.

"Iona call me it's important.

Xx

B"

"What's up?" she said.

"Are you Ok to speak?"

"Yes."

"I got a call this morning from the Ministry refusing my transfer request and telling me to return to Oslo. It seems that they consider government personnel here are at risk. They say it's just for a short time...hello are you still there?"

"I think it's a good idea. I will miss you but it's probably better this way." Iona could hear Bjørge's doorbell ring.

"Hang on."

Still holding the phone Bjørge walked along the hall and opened the door. A man in his late-forties clean shaven wearing sun glasses and a brown cord suit was holding a package.

"Sorry to bother you I have a package for Miss Iona McCallum."

Bjørge held out his hand.

"I'm sorry Miss McCallum has to sign for it herself."

Iona was hearing what was going on and began shouting into the phone.

"CLOSE THE DOOR BJØRGE."

"Who is it from?"

"I don't know mate I'm just the courier and I need her signature."

"Well you're out of luck she's not here."

"CLOSE THE BLOODY DOOR."

"Do you know where I could find her? It may be something valuable in the package."

"I'm sorry I can't help and you'll have to excuse me I'm on the phone." Bjørge closed the door.

"I could hear what was going on and I was shouting down the phone. It's the oldest trick in the book. You should have taken a photograph of him."

"I'm worried about you Iona come with me to Norway."

"I can't."

"Where are you?"

"I'm just coming off Princes Street heading for the offices...sorry Bjørge I can't even tell you where that is. Did you post the package?"

"Yes. I'm really quite upset about all of this."

"I know, I know when this is over we'll be together, I promise. I have to go, love you."

"Elsker deg også."

Iona pressed the red phone icon just as the bus pulled up at her stop. She grabbed her handbag and raced for the door.

Emlyn Llewellyn closed the folder and looked again at the photograph of Iona McCallum on the front cover. The shape of her face was oddly symmetrical and the soft key light smoothed out any lines she may have had on her forehead. She was not vivacious. You wouldn't pick her out in a crowd but pretty in a fresh girl next door kind of way. She had blue eyes that sparkled, a slightly turned up nose. There were signs on the bridge of her nose that she may have worn glasses perhaps she had taken them off for the photograph or maybe she was wearing contact lenses. The stud in her nose was a diamond. She wore very little in the way of make-up with only a suggestion of lipstick and a hint of mischief in the eye that compensated for the lack of a smile. He quite liked the look of her.

"Emlyn."

He looked up at Jane Caddish, the polar opposite of the woman he had just seen in the photograph and blushed as if his thoughts had been read. She was in her late forties and married to the job.

"Emlyn, Sir Cyrus Steele and I know you haven't finished SIS Intelligence Officer Development Programme and you still have the six week Foundation Investigative Training course to go but we're trying to play catch-up. This will be your first case but it is nevertheless a very important one and we're relying on you for a successful outcome. Iona McCallum is in possession of highly classified top secret material and she most certainly can still access our servers until we finish locking her out. We must have her back in London at all costs. Someone's checked out her mother's house and she's not there. You'll have plenty of time to go through her file properly. She is a very intelligent and resourceful woman who has left to join the Scottish Government. We must not allow that. You will travel to Scotland and using this cover identity and story," she passed a thin folder across the desk. "find her and persuade her to return. You will be issued with a phablet linked to your GCHQ contact who will update you with any changes or new information, details are in the folder. You must keep it with you at all times."

"How will I persuade her to return?"

"You will become her friend, her very best friend, her lover whatever it takes." Emlyn blushed again. "What's wrong? I know you're not...?"

"...No, no not at all."

"I'm not asking you to get emotionally involved that is always fraught with difficulty, the idea is to get her emotionally involved. Now your GCHQ contact is Colleen Bentsen she will feed you data in real time to guide you in Aberdeen and update you in the event of any changes. Study your cover identity and story well then destroy the file. Arrangements have been made for you to travel on the train to Edinburgh then on to Aberdeen which will give you time. It leaves Kings Cross in one hour any questions?"

"What happens if I can't persuade her to return to London?"

"Let's cross that bridge if we get to it."

Emlyn stood up and nodded awkwardly then left. Almost immediately an adjoining door opened. In walked a tall well-built man wearing a dark suit and a thin smile and stood at the other side of the desk.

"Did you hear all of that?" Capello nodded. "Oriel you've been passed directly to me by Col. Arthur Douglas the head of SIS no less. That should indicate to you how important this assignment is. Now I know you would normally only be sent to operate outside of the UK but this is an exception. SIS are not aware of your part in this operation and that's how it must remain. There's a tracker in Llewellyn's phablet, God I hate that word, so you will be able to follow him without getting too close. He really thought we would send a complete novice into the field without a senior agent to keep tabs. He was chosen because he is not like field agents we normally send and that may help when he finds her. Iona would spot a regular field agent a mile off. Both of you looking for her gives us two bites of the cherry. She is in possession of critically important information that she has stolen from GCHQ. It is imperative that you find it and her as soon as possible. Now if by some amazing miracle Llewellyn does actually find her first and persuade her to return, all well and dandy you might not be needed however worse-case scenario, she will have to be eliminated. Do you have a problem with that?"

He subconsciously felt the scar on the right side of his neck and shook his shiny bald head.

On the outside it looked just like an old Leith bonded warehouse which indeed was its former function. In the past it had stored millions of pounds of whisky held in oak sherry casks. Iona entered the outer door and stood inside a security vestibule that had a camera looking down at her. There was a swipe card security pad and nothing else no buzzer. She waited but nothing happened. She took out her phone and text, '*I'm here.*' The lock clicked and a large woman with a red face opened the door and stuck out her hand.

"I'm glad you could make it Iona we're absolutely snowed under sorry my name is Grace. Can I see some ID? The face recognition software is on the blink."

Iona fished around inside her bag and produced a passport. Inside the building there were rows of desks and computers interspersed with tall pot plants. Large ceiling fans ran the length of the building turning silently above the operators. She took her coat and scarf off hanging them with the others on an old bentwood coat stand. The people working away were so engrossed on the screens they didn't notice her.

"Now take a seat. I'm a bit short on your profile so let's just run through some things. By the way this company is actually Softwarehouse Ltd but we have had to put all our commercial clients on hold to work exclusively for the Scottish Government. We normally do just about everything, games, personal security corporate back-up and ransomware rescues to mention some but now the brief is entirely different. I'm rambling on what languages do you speak?"

"Oh, fluently? French Spanish, a little German, some Swahili oh and a little bit of Norwegian."

"Ok, that's good," said Grace typing on her keyboard. "Address?"

Iona gave her the address. "Grace I need to talk to someone well er senior in intelligence."

"Here's an ID card, that's me sweetie, Westminster has cut off all traffic we're not even getting foreign Intel and so you're looking at the only independent intelligence processing department that our country has at the moment. Listen that's enough for just now and I have to get on let me show you your desk. There's already a list of job priorities waiting for you. When this slackens off let's sit down and you can update me, ok?"

"Of course, I have an appointment with the Doctor at lunchtime Grace if that's ok it shouldn't take long."

Of course sweetie, nothing serious I hope."

"Oh no, not at all."

Grace went back to her desk. A young red haired guy next to Iona stared at his monitor and spoke to her without looking.

"Don't be fooled by the mumsie act she's as sharp as a tack."

8

"Colin. Is it alright if I call you Colin?" he nodded. "My name is Dr Tremblay and you've been referred to me by your GP Dr Steven."

"You're American."

"Canadian. Do you know why you have been referred?"

"My Doctor thinks I have PTSD."

"Yes, post-traumatic stress disorder and the medication he prescribed is an anti-depressant Phenelzine is that correct?" Colin nodded. "Ok before I begin it's very important for you to understand that the only judgement I will be making is how best to treat you and therefore it is crucial that you are not inhibited in any way. Patient confidentiality is absolute, Ok? Now there are a number of different methods of treating PTSD and in order to tailor that treatment I have to ask some very personal questions that may cause you some distress, Ok? Now can you describe to me first of all why you think you need treatment?"

"I have disturbing flashbacks and I get angry."

"Have you ever felt like hitting someone?"

"Quite often."

"And have you."

Colin thought about the animals in the Well. "I have controls. I hurt two people in the pub the other day. They were threatening some customers."

"Apart from that?"

"No."

"What makes you angry?"

"Many things?"

"Do you try to work out why you're angry?"

"There are times when I know precisely why I get angry that I would consider is fairly normal?..."

"...Such as?"

"Inequalities of life, hypocrisy, enforced poverty, unfair sanctioning..."

"...Sanctioning, what's that?"

"It's when the DWP decide not to pay benefits. Then I have to borrow money from my parents, go to the food bank that kind of thing."

"And other times?"

"At other times when I think about it clearly I have no idea why I feel like that."

"But it's enough to give you cause for concern?"

"Yes."

"Is the Phenelzine helping?"

"Not really."

"You were in the army, for how long?"

"Four years."

"In Iraq and Afghanistan?" Colin nodded. "And in that time you killed people?" He nodded again. "At a distance or close-up?"

"Both."

"How did you feel afterwards?"

"Nothing."

"What?"

"I didn't feel anything. Killing is what you get drilled for it's in the training, like all training it's to stop you thinking about your actions, reactions, not much more than a reflex. There's no time to think. That's the difference between staying alive and ending up in a body bag."

"Have you seen your friends killed in action?"

"Yes."

"Tell me about that."

Colin looked away and felt the anger rising. He had never spoken about his experiences before. He knew that she was doing her job and that it was a necessary part of the healing process, but she didn't realize how painful it was. He could describe to her in great detail courtesy of vivid slow motion flashbacks what the IED did to the snatch Landrover he was following. It wasn't called a mobile coffin for nothing. Mates he had laughed and joked with, fought with, gambled with, felt homesick with, were like brothers. You cannot get closer to a bunch of lads than in the army when death can visit any time. Your life has been saved by them many times and you have saved the lives of others. That's how it works.

"Once, four of us got separated from the platoon doing house to house looking for a high value target. I saw an RPG being launched from a rooftop. I shouted incoming RPG and threw myself behind a wall, there was an explosion. I got up and started firing at figures coming out of the dust and when it cleared I looked around for my mates and they were in bits strewn all over the place."

"How did you feel?"

"Initially, better them than me what do you think of that? I still feel bad thinking about that reaction. That thought lasted for a second or two and then the anger, the waste of good men and then the sadness. It was profoundly sad. I sat down and cried. I wanted to check and see if there was anyone alive but I knew they weren't. I knew what their wives and their girlfriends and children looked like we had often shown each other photographs and I tried not to imagine the hurt that was waiting for them. It was like a part of me inside had died. Then the rest of the guys turned up and I was sent off to the medics for a check."

There was a silence. Dr Tremblay leaned forward and switched off the recorder. She wrote some notes on the margin of a typed A4 sheet and looked at him. His eyes were closed and there was sweat on his upper lip. During her career she had heard things that should never be repeated, things that are so awful they can taint the listener. Even some of her colleagues had needed counselling.

"Colin in case you think I have a dispassionate view of your situation my brother who was in the army suffered PTSD as well. In fact that's what made me want to specialize. This is a very positive start. Let's leave it for now and keep taking the anti-depressants. There will be many sessions longer than this, how many I don't know it depends on your progress but what I do know is that I can help you."

'Forget Aberdeen get off at Edinburgh Waverley.'

Emlyn Llewellyn shrugged his shoulders and put his phone back in his pocket. He hadn't taken long to memorizing his cover story.

'Your name is Renton Powell, a twenty-three year old dropout from Cardiff Law School. You were born in Port Talbot. When you were small you travelled to the coast with Mum Gwyneth, Dad Peter and your two brothers Daffyd two years older that you and Brin the youngest to the holiday caravan in Morfa Nefyn for

three weeks in the summer. You saved Brin from drowning one year when he had got out of his depth in the sea and pulled him onshore. Your interests include the decorative arts, bird watching, hill walking, skiing, classical music and rugby.'

"That's stupid I don't know anything about rugby," he muttered.

'Your father and mother had both been killed in a car crash in Italy while you were in University. Your phobias are fear of heights, enclosed spaces and snakes. Your good at cooking and know your way round the wine cellar.'

Then he read with renewed interest the file on Iona. She was twenty-four, an honour's graduate in Psychology at the School of Psychology & Neuroscience University of St Andrews. She went on to gain her PHD at an early age in Philosophy and Psychology Producing a thesis on the impact of social context on behaviour. She rarely uses the term Doctor. She was an unexpected pregnancy when her parents were in their early forties. Her father left the marital home seeking a divorce. Her mother lives alone in a terraced house in Melville Crescent Edinburgh. She has two sisters living abroad. Her boyfriend is Bjørge Tennfjord a Norwegian national who works as a cultural attaché in the Norwegian embassy in London and has been cleared in a thorough vetting process. His parents are living in Stavanger. Emlyn looked out of the window as the train pulled into Waverley Station. He closed the folder, pushed it into his rucksack and pulled down a suitcase from the rack as the train stopped. He checked his watch and sent a text.

'Arrived at Waverley.'

"I know," said Colleen to her monitor.

9

"How's your Mum?" Dr Elizabeth Winters was washing her hands. She had been the family Doctor for many years.

"A little shaken up I think it's knocked her confidence but she's alright. I've packed her off to the Highlands with her cat in an ambulance."

"Why?"

"Bad things are going to happen especially in the central belt."

"Well let's take care of the here and the now. You haven't been pregnant before have you?"

"No."

"Ok the blood samples the nurse took will test for all kinds of things. I'll just run through the list which is actually quite comprehensive, we don't believe in leaving anything to chance. Complete blood count tests for blood issues like anaemia, HIV, RPR for any sexually transmitted diseases that baby can catch, Rubella, Varicella that's for chickenpox, checks for hepatitis B and you've already given a urine sample, yes?" Iona nodded. "That checks for urinary infections, kidney disease and diabetes. I don't think there is any need for sickle-cell anaemia." The doctor took a smear, labelled it and put it in a sealed bag. "Now I'm going to do a bi-manual internal examination ok?" Iona nodded. "Well, all seems perfectly normal. Now for the really interesting bit, I'm going to use this ultrasound scanner." She said smearing Vaseline onto her abdomen. She watched a small monitor while sliding the scanner around. "Do you have a preference, boy or girl?"

"No not at all but I know it's going to be a boy."

"Mm well I have the happy news that you are most definitely pregnant and as to the baby's sex, it's too early to tell just yet but in either case you are going to have a baby in little under six months' time, congratulations Iona."

The black van with dark tinted windows pulled alongside the security booth in the underground car park. The window lowered just enough for the nozzle of a silencer screwed into a Special Forces issue Sig Sauer P230 pistol to poke out. It spat twice and both guards were on the floor with neat entry wounds to their foreheads.

"We will have to leave First Minister if we are to be on time at the US Consulate, the traffic is building up. We can't keep the American Secretary of State waiting. This is a highly privileged secret meeting that very few countries ever get a chance to have with such a powerful man."

"Don't fuss Henry, we won't be late."

It took seconds to attach the magnetic package fitted with a trembler detonator under the First Minister's car. Release the safety catch and they were gone. Any forward or backward motion would trigger the bomb. Thirty seconds later the chauffeur opened the Mercedes door climbed in and started her up. The first minister came out of the lift with an aide and her personal private secretary and met two armed police bodyguards. Four police motorcyclist were waiting by the Mercedes two at the front and two at the rear. The First Minister was walking towards the car and talking to her husband on the phone.

"Yes John of course I know it's his birthday, could you arrange something for tonight, nothing elaborate my father likes it simple."

She got into the limousine. The door closed and it took off. It exploded before it reached the exit killing everyone inside and seriously injuring the motorcyclists.

Chuck Morales the US foreign Secretary was unnerved by events. "Mr President, it has hit the fan."

"What's happening Chuck?"

"The First Minister of Scotland has just been assassinated, blown up in her car."

"When?"

"We had an appointment for two o'clock, she should have been here now. It was about fifteen minutes ago."

"This is not good, who's behind it?"

"We don't yet it's too early to say but it sounds like it was far too well organised for a bunch of unionist supporters."

"Specifically."

It's just a hunch but the number ten springs to mind, what's our official line."

"Neutral, of course. Appalled at the death of a respected first minister, you know the kind of stuff."

"Ok I know we're in a very delicate position, we'll appeal for calm blah, blah, blah, call for restraint that kind of thing."

"What kind of reaction do you expect to happen?"

"Well it's not going to be good."

"Why?"

"Because there are a lot of people in the US who have very close ties to Scotland, perhaps even more so than the so-called special relationship with the UK."

"So what's going to happen next?"

"The upshot is that there will be a reaction to this from Scotland which of course is the intention. If London use this as an excuse to impose martial law things could very quickly spiral out of control. These are very dangerous times Rob."

"Make your way back home Chuck."

"I'll be flying out as soon as I get to the airport."

"What about the risk to Americans?"

"I don't think it's necessary yet to warn travellers not to come here."

"Or England."

"Yes indeed or England who knows where this will lead."

"I spoke to her yesterday."

"Good is there a transcript?"

"Yes."

"Good if I could get a copy it might help."

"What about the press?"

"I'll have to give some kind of statement at the airport. What worries me is if this whole thing turns into a shoot-out there could be serious implications for the UK, I don't mean just trade sanctions."

"What implications?"

"Scotland could suck in a whole lot of foreign mercenaries for example. I'll be raising this whole business with the French President when I see him later on today. I have no doubt he will be as concerned as we are at this development. Oh by the way Rob I've had a very unsettling conversation with the vice president of Nicaragua, Eleanor MacPherson. She is incandescent with rage about the events in Scotland asking what the US are doing about it. No prizes for guessing why."

Helen Butler checked her monitor under the glass table in the studio. "We have some breaking news. Reports are coming in of an explosion in the basement car park of Holyrood house. Unconfirmed online press agency postings are saying that the First Minister of Scotland Janet Cassie has been killed with a device that appears to have been attached to her car and detonated seconds after it picked her up in the car park basement of Holyrood. An aide and a chauffeur also died in the blast. This is as yet I stress unconfirmed so far. I think we have David McFarlane live outside the building, David this is shocking news if it is correct what is happening at Holyrood right now?"

"Well the building is still being evacuated. We were actually inside waiting to do some interviews and heard a loud bang. Seconds before this live transmission I was handed an update from Police Scotland, the first Minister was on her way to meet the US Foreign Secretary Chuck Morales to discuss many things but ostensibly about Scotland's relations with America as a new sovereign nation. It is almost as if the assassination was timed to prevent this. The names of the others who died have been withheld until the relatives have been informed. Four police motorcyclists were also caught in the blast and taken to hospital one has since died and the other three are in a serious condition. Police Scotland have also said that they have discovered two security staff who were manning the barrier of the car park, shot dead and I quote 'almost in an execution style shooting.' Their names are not being released until the next of kin have been informed. It is understood that the Deputy First Minister Constance Black will assume the responsibility of leading the Scottish

Government and I have just noticed that a van carrying forensic specialists have arrived and are examining the crime scene. Back to you in the studio."

"Thank you David McFarlane. During that live piece from David it has been confirmed that the First Minister of Scotland Janet Cassie has been assassinated. Widespread condemnation of the killing of the First Minister is already streaming in from all over the globe. Many of the world's leaders are responding to the shocking assassination but first we go over to Parliament where the Prime Minister is making a statement to the House."

"Mr Speaker I think I speak for the whole of the House in condemning wholeheartedly this despicable and barbaric act of terrorism. The loss of a young brilliant politician, Janet Cassie will be sorely missed. Our prayers and thoughts go out to family and friends of all of the victims. We will not rest until the perpetrators of this horrific crime are caught and punished. We will stand shoulder to shoulder with Scotland in this time of crisis and that is why we have offered support to the Scottish Government should they ask for it. I would be failing in my duty if I did not point out to the Scottish people that there can be no negotiations regarding independence while there is on-going unrest and the security of the country is at risk. Our priority now is to ensure the safety of all of the Scottish people before anything else."

"That was Prime Minister Charles Keating speaking live at the Houses of Parliament. Messages of sympathy have been flooding in to Bute House from all over Scotland and indeed all over the world as the news travels the globe. President Robert Wallace led the world in condemnation and gave this tribute to the First Minister from the Whitehouse where the Saltire and the American flags are side by side at half-mast."

"Janet Cassie was a highly respected clever politician who understood the importance of being able to communicate with anyone and everyone. She was the patron of many charitable causes in Scotland and in other parts of the world. She was on her way to a meeting with Chuck Morales the Foreign Secretary when the attack took place an attack that may well affect the direction that she wanted to take with her beloved country. This is a time for mourning, a time for calm and a time to allow wounds to heal. I appeal to the Scottish nation not to seek revenge but to build on the foundations laid by Janet Cassie."

"That was a moving tribute to Janet Cassie from the President of the United States recorded a few moments earlier as the story continues to develop. We are getting a live feed from Prestwick where I believe US Foreign Secretary Richard Conway is giving a statement."

"The killing of Janet Cassie is a tragic loss to Scotland and to Scotland's friends in many parts of the world. As the President has said I was about to meet with the First Minister at Bute House when she was killed. The meeting was intended to cement Scottish American relationships in commerce and to pave the way for an independent Scotland to express their hopes and aspirations for the future. There is a special place in the hearts of Americans for the Scottish people and the pain is real. When the time is right I look forward to re-engaging with the Scottish Government and continuing the dialogue."

"Now a reminder of the main story. The shocking news that First Minister Janet Cassie has been assassinated has cause widespread revulsion and anger in Scotland and throughout the world with many messages of sympathy from heads of state. Her husband John Cassie is said to be inconsolable."

Capello loved irony. To be searching for someone innocently accused of stealing what he possessed with the quasi-legal right to kill her was deliciously ironic. He was intending to merely disappear but when the call came he couldn't resist it. Fingers touched the scar. It was his good luck charm. Caused by a near silent polymer cased 9mm subsonic bullet from a Glock 17 it narrowly missed his main artery leaving its mark. It gave him comfort knowing that his time was not yet up. It was also ironic that he should be in Scotland hunting a nationalist. His family roots were in Catalan, a country desperately trying to break free from Spanish rule. He looked at the screaming headlines of the early evening Edinburgh newspaper '*POLICE HUNT FOR ASSASSINS*' and smiled. The special forces unit from A squadron was already back at base in Hereford. He folded his paper took a sip of chilled fruit juice and looked around the Bistro Bar.

People were beginning to pour in from various local offices for an after work drink. He checked the signal from the Welshman cursing control for using a complete amateur who couldn't catch a cold never mind an intelligence analyst who had gone off radar. This was a complete waste of time, he should be hunting her himself not shadowing a hapless wannabe. He hadn't known about the plan to assassinate the First Minister and it meant nothing to him, of course it needed something major to start the ball rolling. They liked to keep him in the dark about many things. He hadn't been told precisely what was so special about Iona McCallum for example because there was no need to know. But of course he knew. It didn't matter he had seen it all before. He had spent a lot of time in some of the most unstable corrupt countries in the world dodging bullets and to date had never failed to achieve his mission.

Control was flailing in the dark, they couldn't be sure that McCallum was in Edinburgh. He left the Bistro and headed along Hanover Street to George Street where a demonstration was taking place. Hundreds of youths looking like skinheads of old waving union Jacks hurled abuse at counter demonstrators waving the Saltire. The inevitable clash happened with police failing to keep them apart. He stopped at a doorway and watched the proceedings unfold, it was carefully choreographed. Bricks and stones began flying through the air catching Nationalists off guard and injuring some police. He looked at his watch, it was only a matter of minutes before the riot squad would arrive to disperse the crowd. He went into the shop and pretended to be interested in the tourist tat, tartan Nessie's, haggis in a kilt and so on. It was so kitsch and naff he was tempted to buy something to take back so he picked up a miniature set of tartan bagpipes with an I heart Scotland label stuck on when a rock hit the window shattering it.

An elderly American couple screamed in fear and ran towards the staff at the rear of the shop while he looked out through the gaping hole unmoved. A flash of annoyance crossed his face and left just as quickly. Two young men came in with scarves over their faces and picked up the till. His pet hate was looting. He shook his head and picked up a three wood from a rack of golf clubs and lashed out at the back of their legs. They howled dropping the till, fell to the ground rolling around then got up. They looked back in surprise and hobbled out leaving the till. He picked it up and put it back on the counter checked the label on the bagpipes and placed seven pounds thirty-six pence next to the till. Outside, the riot squad had arrived and the demonstrators had moved along George Street still fighting with Nationalists. He waved at the small group at the back of the shop and left.

10

The double decker bus stopped at the junction of Hanover Street and George Street held up by the demonstration. Iona sat upstairs at the very front with a ringside seat of the action below. She was eating a small bag of pickled onions. She noticed a shop window being smashed and two men wearing scarves running in. She took her phone out and began recording video. The two men reappeared hobbling away from the shop followed shortly after by a tall bald man in an immaculate dark blue suit. He was carrying some kind of tartan souvenir. He stared after the two men, turned and walked down towards Princess Street. Iona was still in shock at the news about the First Minister and what was happening in front of her was just an emotional blur. She stopped filming and took another onion enjoying the sharp vinegar taste.

The bus made a detour and instead of travelling along George Street turning down towards Princess Street. There was no sign of the bald headed man. Having travelled the length of Princess Street the bus stopped at the bus station where she got off. She pulled up the zip of her coat against a cold wind that met her, the first sign of the end of summer. It was a short walk to Dottie Jāyah's basement flat who had offered her a spare bed for as long as she wanted. Dottie had been sent from Malaya by her wealthy parents to study medicine at St Andrews where she became good friends with Iona but had lost touch. Iona had once mistakenly called her Dorothy and Dottie explained that her name was in fact Malaysian and meant gift of God. She unlocked and pushed open the heavy door closing it behind her. She paused, it was strangely quiet. A tingle of fear made her shudder.

Dottie said she would be in but just in case had given her a spare key. There was very little ambient light in the hall. Iona looked for the light switch and flicked it on. Two pretend stained glass shades lit up the hall.

She took off her coat and hung it on the oak hall-stand next to a colourful collection of raincoats. "Hello," she said not expecting a reply. It served to break the tension. She walked passed two closed doors and continued along the hall her footsteps echoing on the solid parquetry floor. She glanced up at a framed copperplate engraving hanging on an egg shell blue wall of Alexander III of Scotland being rescued from the fury of a stag. She paused to put her handbag on an oak hall chair then stopped at a bevelled glass panelled kitchen door. She peered through the closed door. The kitchen was modern and tidy with a small dining table at one end and on one of the chairs lay a sleeping stuffed, knitted cat. She touched the door handle and at that moment the letterbox on the front door slammed shut. Startled she turned to see a newspaper lying on the mat. She went back along the hall and bent down to pick it up when the door opened.

"Hi, sorry I'm a little late there was a sudden emergency that I had to deal with, some minor injuries from the demonstration on George Street."

"Not at all I've just arrived," said Iona.

Dottie went through to the kitchen and picked out a Waitrose ready meal from a shopping bag, switched on the oven and put it in.

"Now let me show you around." She said taking off her coat and leaving it on the back of a chair. "This is the sitting room," she said opening a door and switching on the light.

The parquetry flooring continued into the room where to the left a large red sofa below an impressive harbour seascape painting by John Bellany faced the window to the right. In the centre a tiled Victorian fireplace held a gas, fake coal fire and above there was an over-mantle inset with a mirror. In front of the window was a large Bonheur de Jour with French Kingwood marquetry and ormolu mounts to the cabriole legs. On it was a Dell 17 inch laptop.

"You know I don't spend a lot of time here that's why I didn't bother getting a television set. The hours are incredibly long at the A & E, still another year and I can move on. Would you like a drink, a glass of white maybe?"

"No, if you've got something soft that would be perfect. Have you decided what you are going to do next Dottie?"

"I think I might stay and work in Scotland, maybe specialize in Paediatrics boring eh? Let's talk about you."

Dottie took out a pack of orange juice and a bottle of wine from the fridge, found two glasses in a cupboard, put them on the table and poured out the drinks. She sat down and blew a strand of hair from her face.

"What a day. I heard you're working in London."

"Yes, well was, not now. Normally I'd stay at Mum's house but I can't at the moment, it's very good of you to put me up."

One of the things that Iona liked about Dottie was that she didn't pry and seemed to have an inbuilt mechanism that avoided asking awkward questions.

"I don't think you met my boyfriend Bjørge, he's had to go back to Norway which is a bit of a pain."

"And?"

Iona giggled. "No-one knows yet, can't keep it from a Doctor."

Dottie squealed and gave her a hug.

"Look this is going to sound like I've got a severe case of paranoia and I'm not going to be able to explain myself but bear with me. It's a good idea that nobody knows I'm here. Not even Bjørge knows where I am. I think there will be somebody from London looking for me. So I would be very grateful if my name doesn't appear on any social media, emails and texts. Is that ok?"

"Of course. What on earth would they do if they found you?"

"I don't know. If I thought for a minute that I was placing you in danger I wouldn't be here. Thanks for letting me stay Dottie you're a pal. What about you are there any consultants taking your fancy?" she asked changing the subject.

"Yes but they've all been caught early. Although there is one single guy who's cute, he's from Ethiopia."

"Is it true that you're related to Malayan aristocracy?"

"So my father keeps telling me, he has a lineage chart and I'm supposedly in line to be a princess if certain people die but I think I would have to be a hundred and thirty years old for that to happen or start a family cull."

"So you want to be a Paediatrician?"

"Sometimes and then again I think maybe I'd like to go into private practice. You know what? My future will show itself when the time comes and then the choice per se won't exist because it will be glaringly obvious. That's what I'm clinging on to in a vain attempt to avoid making any decisions, does that make sense?"

"I have a problem with that. If you have hard-wired DNA doesn't that limit your choices?"

"Who knows? Not a bad thing some times. Iona if you want you could fly to Kuala Lumpur my family would look after you."

"I wouldn't be allowed to board the flight, anyway what would I do in exile?"

"What's going to happen to Scotland?"

"Ultimately? Freedom of sorts. But there is going to be a lot of heartache en-route, no doubt. There's a lot going on but despite that, the clock can never be turned back." The oven pinged signalling that the chicken Rendang with potatoes was cooked.

Llewellyn looked down from his rented flat on the corner of London Street and Drummond Place. The empty cobbled street below glistened in the failing light reflecting the newly lit street lamps. Someone was walking a dog in the patchy oasis of greenery and trees that the street encircled. He was feeling lonely, missing his friends in London who he couldn't even contact and there was a creeping cloud of depression hanging over him that he was trying to shake off. He took another swig of beer and gazed over the Edinburgh skyline. He wondered how on earth he was supposed to find someone who didn't want to be found amongst a million people. She might not even be in the city or she could live round the corner. His single glazed large sash window vibrated a little as a taxi sped by. Why bother looking for a woman he's not going to find, he might as well just enjoy himself, do a bit of sight-seeing, visit the Castle, the National Museum of Scotland, have a wander around the West End Village, spoilt for choice really.

But he knew he couldn't, his conscience wouldn't allow it. He took another swig. It was almost dark now. He allowed the gloom to fill the room leaving the lights off. He took out a laptop lay on the sofa and opened it logging in. He could just make out his reflection in the monitor, his beard needed a trim and he could do with a haircut, maybe tomorrow he thought. He clicked on a search engine and waited for it to appear. There was an ache of sorts nagging him and he closed eyes trying to work out why. He thought for a while but couldn't find any reason why he felt like that. Colleen would be home now, he could only contact her out of hours in an emergency. He checked his email client but there was nothing new. He finished his beer and left the bottle on the floor. The bluish light from the laptop on his chest dimmed as he closed his eyes again and went into standby.

11

Capello breathed in deeply and exhaled slowly. His eyes were closed though there was no light in the room with the curtains drawn. The Remington Modular Sniper Rifle parts lay on the table. He touched each one in turn burning an image in his mind as to their positions on the table. When he was satisfied he put both hands behind his head with one palm reassuringly touching the scar. He cleared his mind of all thoughts, clicked a stopwatch and began assembling the rifle piece by piece in the correct order. To empty the mind and default to an automatic reflex was not something that came naturally. The key was practice. It was only after hours of training and self-discipline that he could achieve the assembly. He didn't have to think about it in the same way a classical guitarist doesn't think of which order to pluck the strings. It was through repetition and training. The rifle was complete and he stopped the watch. He opened his eyes and saw the green glow from the face of the stopwatch needle resting at ninety-nine seconds that was his best time ever. Lightning silently lit the sky and penetrated through the curtains into the room. A feeling of intense satisfaction swept over him accompanied by a rush of adrenalin that he always mastered control over. A body perfect, a mind perfect, he welcomed the disciplines that led to achievements. There was a certain artistry in his profession when a Remington MSR could kill at almost a mile away but it needed the disciplines he possessed. They say that the recipient of an MSR .338 Lapua Magnum round never hears the shot that kills.

Llewellyn sat bolt upright on the sofa and shouted, "Yes, yes, yes."

The laptop slid off and landed on the floor coming off standby. He picked it up put the living room light on and placed the laptop on the coffee table rubbing his hands together. He entered Police Scotland's main servers searching for CCTV control Edinburgh and found it. He then took a feed linking the hundreds of images through GCHQ face recognition servers.

"Llewellyn you're a genius," he said.

He filtered the search and pasted a copy of Iona's photograph. If she was in Edinburgh it would be only a matter of time before her face would be recognized alerting him. The only down side was the time lag. It could take up to an hour for confirmation and Iona could travel quite a long distance in an hour but it was better than nothing. He looked at his watch, it was only 4.20am. He took his laptop through to the bedroom plugging the power in, lay down on the bed and immediately fell asleep.

Something woke Llewellyn up. It was light. He looked at his watch showing 8.30am. There was that funny sound again, the same sound that had woken him up. His laptop on the bedside table was flashing. He swung his legs over and stared in disbelief it had worked, he had found her. She was spotted going into the American Diner by a Frederick Street CCTV camera. He texted '*found her*' and hurriedly washed his face brushed his teeth and hair, grabbed a coat and his phone and stormed downstairs out onto the street. There was no sign of a cab so he began to run. Frederick Street wasn't really that far but some of it was up hill and it wasn't long before he was breathing heavily.

Capello intercepted his text and seeing Llewellyn was on the move packed his MSR into a specially made case and followed the signal.

Llewellyn arrived outside the Diner breathing hard. He looked inside noticing all the booths lining the windows were full. He couldn't see any further inside because of the reflection. He entered and looked around. It was busy with only a couple of empty tables and then he caught sight of Iona. His heart started racing. He waited trying to compose himself. She was recognizable even with glasses on. Her photograph hadn't done her any favours she was gorgeous. She was looking at her mobile while buttering a piece of toast. He walked over to her and looked around then back at her. His heart was pounding.

"It's busy is it ok if I sit here?" his face was flushed. Iona shrugged. "Thanks," he took off his jacket and placed it on the seat back. He looked at her again but she appeared to be ignoring him. He got up and went over to the counter and asked for a Cappuccino.

"I'll bring it over, dear."

He sat down again thinking hard about how to break the ice. All his chat up lines seemed stale and embarrassing. He thought about 'have we met before?' But couldn't bring himself to deliver such a corny line. The woman from the counter arrived at the table with his Cappuccino. Llewellyn moved to take the coffee when the teaspoon fell from the saucer, bounced off the table and landed on Iona's partially eaten fried egg.

"Oops I am so sorry how clumsy of me let me order you another egg."

She looked at him properly for the first time as his face reddened and smiled. "No it's fine I've finished anyway." She smiled again turned to her phone and then glanced up again. "You're staring."

"Am I? Oh sorry." He retrieved his teaspoon wiped it on a serviette and added some sugar to his coffee. "This is my first time in Edinburgh I'm flat sitting for a couple of friends who have gone on holiday. My name's Renton, my friends call me Rent boy? You know Train Spotting?" He held out his hand which she ignored. "This is my first trip to Edinburgh," he said again unabashed while withdrawing his hand. "It's an exciting place, not like Port Talbot...I'm from Wales..." Iona smiled and returned to her phone. Llewellyn took out his mobile and studied it wondering what to say next.

Capello looked at the American Diner then up and down the street. Opposite the Diner was an insurance building with a flat roof. He quickly unlocked a caretaker's door and climbed the stairs until he reached a door leading onto the roof. He unpacked the MPR and assembled it checking the Schmidt Bender PMII 3-20×50 H2CMR precision scope. Lying down next to a dwarf wall he used the scope to search the Diner until he saw her with Llewellyn. He changed the focus sharpening the image, the cross-hairs met at Iona's head. He took in a deep breath and slowly released the safety catch.

Llewellyn had started babbling on about being a Uni dropout and about life in Wales largely ignored by Iona when he suddenly stopped. A large white van had drawn up outside and the driver had got out and briskly walked away. Iona looked at Llewellyn wondering what had caught his attention. There was a puff of smoke from inside the van. Llewellyn threw himself at Iona knocking over the table and ending up on the floor just as the shock-wave hit the windows. A wall of flame and glass entered the Diner. Those who were seated by the windows were thrown across the room followed by jagged glass shards flying everywhere indiscriminately. Iona and Llewellyn were protected by the table and by being on the floor but others were not so lucky. Families, parents, children and the elderly were not spared. There was blood and glass everywhere. The counter had gone and there was no sign of the waitress.

Above and opposite the building a finger on a trigger with 3.5lbs of pressure of the sniper's rifle was being squeezed gently when the blast went off below. Capello cursed as a cloud of dust and smoke enveloped him. He coughed and spluttered as the acrid smoke entered his lungs.

There was an eerie silence in what was left of the diner and then the screams and awful wailing of those who were still alive and injured. "Are you ok? Are you ok?" he repeated louder.

"I can't hear properly but I'm alright," she said coughing.

"Let's get out of here." He helped her up, picked up his jacket and discovered his phone had gone in the explosion. He grabbed her arm. "No the back way." They went through the kitchens and a doorway that led to an alley. Ambulances with loud sirens were arriving. They took a deep breath of fresh air and walked swiftly out of the area.

When the dust cleared Capello wiped the scope lens with a cloth and searched inside the Diner. All he could see was the dead and dying covered in dust and debris but there was no sign of Iona or Llewellyn. It was time to go.

"There's ringing in my ears," said Llewellyn.

"Mine too."

Iona put the palm of her hands on her tummy and closed her eyes searching for some assurance that everything was still ok. There was no bruising or tenderness, no pain or ache, she didn't even feel in shock because it had happened so quickly. She looked at Llewellyn who was busy blowing the dust out of his nose with a handkerchief.

"We should have tried to help someone."

"The ambulances are here now."

"You saved my life," said Iona shaking the dust from her hair.

"You've lost your glasses."

"I have another pair."

"Let's go and find a quiet place for a coffee."

"No I have to work." She looked at him then gave him a hug. "If it wasn't for you I would be dead."

"Can I see you again?"

"See me again, why?"

"Because we've just had a near death experience together, because I don't know anyone in Edinburgh, because it's going to be a long fortnight and because I think you're very attractive. Not necessarily in that order."

"There is no you me thing. I have a partner who I intend to marry, and I'm really grateful for what you've done honestly, but there is no we or us and there never will be."

He put up his hands. "Sorry, you're quite right. Tell you what, how about being my guide for one evening? Debt paid."

Iona smiled. "You know what? You were coming onto me really strong in the diner and there was no need to sit next to me, there were empty tables. And there's something else that puzzles me Renton." She checked her phone was still working. "You've not asked what my name is."

A tiny alert had been flagged up, just enough to start the thinking process about the circumstances she found herself in. There was something about Renton that didn't quite gel. Perhaps she was getting paranoid but as they say, paranoia might annoy ya but it aint gonna kill ya. She needed time to check him out. If there was something about this guy, she would have to act quickly.

Llewellyn scratched his beard and raised his eyes to the sky. "Your name...of course that was going to be my next question."

"It's Iona. Ok I will, just one night I mean evening but there are conditions," he nodded. "Where are you living?" He told her. "Ok this is important." She handed him a hundred pounds. "Don't go back there, check in at the Travelodge in St Mary's Place and pay for a day room with this. You'll have to get out before seven. Meet me at the Dominion Restaurant in Rose Street at seven. Don't contact anybody, promise Renton, nobody."

Llewellyn laughed. "You're a very strange woman...in the nicest possible way of course. Firstly you don't want to have anything to do with me and then you give me all this money for a room, I don't understand. It's very generous of you but I really don't need the money?"

"It's a loan. I have my reasons and if I'm right I'll explain it to you tonight."

"London has imposed martial law in Scotland with a curfew starting at the weekend and they are also dissolving the Scottish Parliament."

Acting First Minister Constance Black, dark under the eyes, shook her head. Her staff in the small room looked on anxiously.

"The explosion in Frederick Street was the perfect excuse. The bombers were targeting three ministerial cars in a convoy that change route seconds before the blast. All public buildings are to be closed and displaying the Saltire will be a criminal offence. We're being kicked out of Bute House. London is effectively going to run Scotland so we need to be organised. That means that most of you will appear to have gone home. I will be setting up an action Cabinet. Troops that are being confined to barracks will be allowed to leave minus their weapons, we will organize them. It will be necessary to keep the cabinet small with one aim and one aim only, to change the mind of the Westminster Government whatever that takes. I have already recalled all our MP's from London in protest to this decision and we have appealed to the United Nations. It is only a matter of time before political arrests begin. The problem is that without hard evidence proving all this was manufactured by No 10, we are in a very weak position. I want to thank you all for the hard work you have done."

"First Minister the TV cameras are waiting."

She rose from the table and went into an adjoining room with a desk facing four cameras. She looked at the floor manager as the sound recordist tapped the microphones on the desk. When the sound man was satisfied the floor manager counted her down.

"These are grave times for the people of Scotland. London has dismantled a democratically elected government and imposed direct rule. But I do not want to inflame passions that will result in even more deaths. The answer lies in political dialogue, diplomacy and a return to democratic principles. However we are in a situation where social order is threatened where many Scots understandably believe that a forceful and bloody reaction to the decisions taken by the English prime Minister and his colleagues would focus the minds of those who have imposed Westminster rule in Scotland. This is wrong. I appeal to everyone for restraint and calmness. This is a time to be strong in mind and strong in spirit, we will prevail. History has taught a harsh lesson you cannot subjugate a population without destroying it. We will not let that happen. There are countries that are deeply concerned at the unfolding of events. Countries that are emotionally, culturally and spiritually close to Scotland are offering friendship and support. For those families and friends who have lost loved ones their deaths will not be in vain. We will pursue those responsible. Finally I give my solemn pledge to each and every one of you in four simple words. We will be free."

12

"It's me."

"Go on."

"They're both dead."

"The hunted and the hunter?"

"Yes."

"What happened?"

"Somehow he managed to find her."

"How?"

"I don't know, he wasn't as stupid as I thought he was. They both died in the American Diner explosion."

"Are you sure?"

"Of course I'm sure, I had her in my sights. I was just about to pull the trigger when the explosion happened and when the air cleared only a few seconds later, there was nothing except a pile of bodies covered in dust, roof tiles and glass. Nobody could have survived that blast."

"What about the hospital, any sign of them there?"

"I've checked the body count and the list of victims taken to hospital. There was nothing but then you wouldn't expect the Scottish government to release details of the death of a GCHQ security analyst and a field agent for SIS."

"Are you absolutely certain?"

"Yes. There were only seven survivors from the Diner that were taken to hospital and they're all on the critical list and in intensive care, so there's not a chance that these two are still alive."

"Good, let me think."

"So what now?."

"I want to be a hundred percent certain. Stay in Edinburgh for now."

"Why, I told you they're dead and there's no signal from his phone so there's a very good chance that he and his phone and the girl are in pieces in the morgue."

"I don't like to rely on chance. Stay there."

"You really want me to hang around here because frankly I think it's pointless."

"Check out his flat."

"What? Ok if you say so."

Iona was sick. She wasn't sure if it was a delayed effect from the adrenalin after the bombing or the baby. There was some uneasiness inside her and she didn't know why. It was as if she had lost control of something but what? She looked in the mirror and wiped the corner of her mouth with a tissue. She had to make sure he wouldn't contact the outside world but how? He would have to stay where she could keep an eye on him. There was something about him. It wouldn't do any harm to be a guide for one night would it? Damn it, one evening. He was quite good looking in a bohemian non-conformist way. He seemed quite young but looks can be deceptive. Why was he breathless when he sat down at the Diner? She put in her contact lenses and peered at herself in the mirror. Perhaps she should ask Bjørge about this guide business but that would mean telling him that she was nearly blown up. Why do things have to be so damn complicated? She wearily walked into the open plan office and sat down at her desk.

"Iona where have you been? There was an explosion in Frederick Street. Everyone else came in early."

"I was there Grace."

"What? In the Diner?"

"Yes."

"How, you're not even scratched?"

"It's a long story, Grace we really do need to talk. I have ..."

"...Later we need to find out who is behind all of this. Are you ok? I really need you here." Iona nodded.

Llewellyn Arrived at the hotel and paid cash in advance for the day room. It was comfortable with a large King-size bed dominating the room, an armchair at a desk facing a mirror on the wall. He showered and dried himself and lay on the bed wondering why he was here. It had all happened so quickly and Iona had a way of stamping her authority. Something he was used to from his mother. He thought about calling her or Jane Caddish from the room phone but there was something empowering about people thinking you were dead. It felt strange but exciting and then there was Iona, she really was gorgeous and he had a date tonight. His pulse quickened. He would take her back to London and explain that the reason he had not contacted base was that he had to win her trust. Llewellyn knew he was a lousy liar and that he couldn't look her straight in the eye and tell her he hadn't been in contact when he had, so he just had to mark time.

Capello watched the elderly couple at the main door of the block of flats. The man leaning against an unkempt hedge, the woman holding onto a trolley bag for support. They were talking and laughing enjoying each other's company and in no hurry. He waited patiently across the road in a closed butcher shop doorway. Eventually they departed in opposite directions. The door had been left ajar allowing him in. He climbed the stairs to the third floor and quietly let himself into Llewellyn's flat. He took off his shoes and walked across the varnished wooden floored hallway with his hand touching the pistol in its shoulder holster. He checked out the bedroom containing a fitted wardrobe and an unmade double bed with Llewellyn's bag half open next to a rumpled pillow. Inside were a set of fresh clothes and a pair of trainers. The white tiled bathroom was just wide enough for the sink and the bath with a shower hose attached to the taps. On a glass shelf over the sink was a half squeezed tube of toothpaste, a toothbrush, hand-wash and comb. The kitchen looked like it had never been used. He opened some cupboards and found a rubbish bag containing empty beer bottles and sandwich wrappers. The living room had a modernist rug on the wooden floor. Llewellyn's laptop was where he had left it in his rush to leave. Capello picked it up and opened it to see the user password curser blinking. He sat down, closed the laptop and put on his shoes. It looked like Llewellyn had left in a hurry and wasn't coming back.

Llewellyn was waiting outside but not for long when Iona arrived. The Dominium was packed probably because of the impending curfew the following night. They were shown to a table next to the kitchen door and took their seats. Llewellyn looked around the busy restaurant while Iona studied the menu.

"What are you going to have, you haven't looked at the menu?"

"You choose," he said.

She laughed "That's absurd I have no idea what you like."

"That's ok I'll have the same as you, I'm sure you have impeccable taste."

"Ok for starters I'm going to have deep fried Calamari with garlic and..."

"...Calamari what's that?"

"Squid."

"Octopus?"

"Same family."

"I hate octopus," he said picking up the menu.

The waiter was hovering with a notepad taking their orders and it seemed in no time the food arrived. Llewellyn insisted on a different wine for each course and the ambient noise in the restaurant increased in relation to the amount of alcohol taken. Iona told him she wasn't drinking but it made no difference. He poured the wine that stayed untouched in her glasses. Llewellyn talked through his cover story embellishing it here and there and he was pleased he could actually make her laugh. She was enjoying herself. Bjørge was sometimes not frivolous enough. At the end of the meal he discreetly disappeared to pay and returned to the table. "Where to now?" he said, "the night is young."

"You're not at all curious about me," she said with a smile, "isn't that odd?"

"I've been talking about myself too much."

"Could it be that you already know quite a bit about me *Renton*, what is your real name?"

He smiled and attempted to take her hand but she pulled away. "I don't understand, what makes you think I'm someone else?"

"I checked you out and as you know what I do, that shouldn't surprise you."

He picked up the white linen napkin and waved it in the air. "I surrender," he said letting it drop on the table. My name is Emlyn Llewellyn but I am Welsh and I have been sent to persuade you to return to London."

"Jane Caddish gave you my file."

"Yes, this is embarrassing my first field job and I've been rumbled."

"It doesn't make sense."

"What?"

"You being sent. A young inexperienced agent with the brief to persuade me to go back to London, exactly how were you going to do that?"

"Well first I save you from a terrorist bomb and then you are so grateful that you fall in love with me and follow me back to London. Something like that apart from the bomb."

Iona laughed out loud and noticed that Llewellyn was blushing. "I'm sorry, I know operations and Jane Caddish well and there is a piece of the jigsaw missing. Are you working with someone in Edinburgh?"

"No."

"Who is your contact?"

"Colleen Bentsen."

"I don't know her, have you sent in a report today?"

"No."

"Really?"

"I gave you my word."

She touched his hand. "Renton, I mean Emlyn I'm sorry but you make a lousy field agent you really ought to be doing something else. Colleen would have known that you were in the Diner when it blew up."

"Us."

"What? How?"

"I hacked into Police Scotland's Edinburgh CCTV and linked the images through a server with face recognition and I text Colleen when your name came up. I was out of breath having run all the way to the Diner. I didn't know anything about the bomb and I certainly wouldn't put my safety or anybody else's at risk."

"So they think we're both dead."

"Yes."

"That's good."

"How were you so sure about me? The firm are very good at cover story stuff."

"They are but I'm very good at what I do. Renton Powell drowned in a swimming pool in Marbella when he was three years old in 1999. His body was taken home to Cardiff and buried at the Western Cemetery. Classic cover stories mostly start in cemeteries. You'll have to stay with me now you can't go back to your place? And Em I really need to trust you." He nodded.

I'll pay for the meal," she said getting her purse out.

"No I've already paid."

"What with?"

"Damn," he said. "My debit card."

Iona closed her eyes and shook her head. "Let's get out of here, you and I have got some serious talking to do about our respective futures."

13

"Ma'am it's Colleen, Llewellyn's debit card has just paid for a meal at Dominium's restaurant in Edinburgh."

"Could it be him?"

"Could be, but I know for sure, somebody used it."

"How much?"

"£145. I guess he wasn't alone."

"Capello this is Jane, there is a strong possibility that Llewellyn is alive go to the Dominion restaurant he may still be there check the CCTV if he's gone."

"Your days with SIS are over now that your cover is blown," said Iona stopping at a cash machine.

"Probably, what are we doing here?"

Iona handed him a pen and a scrap of paper. "Write your pin down."

She took it back and wrote '*help yourself*' and wedged it into a corner of the machine. They walked a few yards on where a couple of guys were standing smoking.

"Someone's left a card in the cash machine have you lost one?"

Both looking startled nodded and ran off to the machine.

"That'll confuse London for a while."

"Dottie I'm not going to be able to explain anything," Iona apologised, "but would it be alright if Emlyn stayed with us for a few days?"

"Of course, do want me to make a bed in the spare room or..."

"Oh it's nothing like that, spare room is fine thank you. You might hear some pretty strange conversations so just ignore what we're saying. Thanks Dottie. Ok Em some house rules, no wandering around at night, no using Dottie's phone and treat Dottie with the utmost respect, get it?"

"Got it."

"Good, now I have to go to work tomorrow so it's early for a simple breakfast and we'll go over a plan."

"What plan?"

"I haven't got one yet."

"Do you have any CCTV?"

"No."

Capello winced. "Could you give me a description of what they looked like?"

"Look around you pal we're absolutely hoochin in here I couldn't even tell you who all the staff are."

"But it was a couple."

"Sorry pal I've got far too much on my plate."

The under manager left him texting. '*Nothing, not here, no CCTV.*' He received a reply.

'*£300 taken from cash machine on George Street/Hanover Street*'

He rushed out of the door almost knocking over a waiter and sprinted along the street. He stood by the deserted cash machine breathing heavily and heard his text ping.

'*Card used in an off-licence on York Place*'

He arrived at the off-licence and flashed an ID card. "Did you have a couple in using a card within the last twenty minutes?"

"Yes, a couple of dodgy looking characters."

"What?"

"Yeah and they bought the most expensive whisky we have, two bottles."

"We believe that card may have been stolen by the couple is your CCTV working?"

"Of course but why do you keep calling them a couple it was two young guys." He looked at Capello's neck. "That must have been painful."

"What?"

"The scar on your neck must have been painful."

"Oh yeah."

"How did you get it?"

"By not minding my own business."

The shopkeeper wound back the video to show two hooded young men. He couldn't make out their faces clearly but they were most definitely not Llewellyn and McCallum. He went out of the shop and text.

The two are dead, stolen card was being used by two youths. Put a stopper on the card.

He put his phone in his pocket and froze. In the near distance, possibly two or three streets away were the unmistakable sounds of gunfire, possibly a Glock 26 or a Walther P99. He instinctively padded the concealed Heckler & Koch USP pistol. He had used it many times in foreign countries since he was recruited into the Increment and always felt vulnerable without it.

"When's the baby due?"

"You're observant."

"Not really, refusing drink last night and being sick in the bathroom this morning was a bit of a clue."

Llewellyn was helping himself to a cereal and had a lopsided grin on his face.

"End of February. I've been thinking, if the card trick worked London would have to assume that we are both dead."

"I've decided. I don't want to be dead I want to go back to London and resume my career."

"In what, SIS? There is one way to get back your identity but it means that you would have to be a double agent."

"I can't be a double agent I'm not even good at being a single agent."

"Just a thought."

There was a carefully orchestrated silence punctuated with crunching serial from Llewellyn.

"Go on," he said.

"You turn up at the A&E having lost your memory and then miraculously part of it comes back but you don't remember anything about the explosion or me. Then you go back to London and start feeding Intel to us. How about it?"

"I don't know. If they found out I could be genuinely dead."

"Look stay here, don't move I'll speak to my supervisor, we'll sort something out. Don't contact anyone, the email I got from Jane Caddish was very threatening and I don't understand why. I need time to work out what's going on...please."

"Grace there's a shipment of arms and explosives heading north towards Scotland."

"Good girl where is it?"

"Darlington. The vehicle is a white pantechnicon with Wiley's removals on the side."

Grace emailed the information to operations. "Where on earth did you get that from Iona?"

"It's what I was trying to tell you, I still have access to Cheltenham servers."

"How come you should have been locked out?"

"Their servers are not flawless and I know one or two flaws that allow me access and I suspect Jane Caddish might have guessed that. She's very smart. It could be why she desperately wants me back. But others have left without this nonsense. There's something else by the way I wasn't alone in the American Diner. An agent from SIS found me. I suspected he was a spook but didn't have it confirmed until last night. He spotted the bomb just before it went off and saved my life. He had the standard cover story that was easy to unpick and he admitted it. So now London thinks we're both dead."

"Where is he now? He could be useful."

Iona laughed. "Useless more like. He's dithering. I'm trying to turn him and send him back to London. Why they sent a novice on his own beggars' belief. He's at Dottie's. He needs to be chaperoned is there anyone in ops?"

"No everyone is stretched to the max. He'll have to stay with you. The curfew starts tonight there could be a lot of trouble on the streets. There's a great deal of resentment building up it's almost as if London wants to provoke violence."

"I heard gunfire last night. It's getting quite serious Grace."

"I think it's going to get a whole lot worse before it gets better. London is beginning to shut down the main ISPs. There are only a handful of small independents that might continue and they could find themselves being targeted. They are trying to stop people communicating. We'll be alright we have satellite links. There is going to be a big protest rally in George Square on the hour of the curfew and in Princess Street. The next thing will be tanks on the streets. Scottish regiments have been confined to barracks but the Royal Scots Guards are going to take orders from the First Minister. A large aircraft carrier is arriving in the Clyde later on today from the Med with more combat troops flying to Prestwick on one of three C-17A Globe-master III's. The other two are destined for Edinburgh and Aberdeen. It's heating up."

"Troops are not trained for crowd control or riots that's crazy."

"They've relocated armed drones from the Middle-East to bases like RAF Waddington we don't know what they're operational duties will be. Are you ok you're looking a bit flushed?"

"I'm fine."

"The First Minister is determined not to mobilize the Royal Scots Guards to protect the population fearing that it will make things worse but I think London has all the excuses they need. Tonight there will be a large number of politicians who intend to speak at the rally in a direct stand against the curfew and the escalating violence. If they are arrested and imprisoned it could mean civil war spilling over the border. You could argue that the irony of road blocks at the border between Scotland and England is hardly conducive to integrating Scotland back into the UK. Can you try to get anything on their plans?"

"They've already blocked me from two servers but there are another three that I think I can still access. The information that goes through the department I used to work for doesn't usually handle clandestine ops. But there has been a lot of analysis processed on the infrastructure of Scotland ranging from various methods of power generating, nuclear, gas, oil, wind, solar and tidal and also the transport infrastructure and much more. So they're not for fun, they are deadly serious about bringing Scotland to heel even if it means crippling parts of our infrastructure. There is someone that has popped up a couple of times in the chatter. Does the name Capello mean anything to you?" Grace shook her head.

"Mr Raknar Aalto The President of the European Parliament has warned the British government that there could be serious consequences if the considerable military build-up of troops in Scotland continues giving rise to instability and with the possible danger of civil war. 'The European Union cannot stand by and see a former member of the EU that wishes to remain in Europe subjected to this threat,' he said and called on NATO to intervene. The President of America Robert Wallace has called for dialogue and calm. 'The tensions in the region must be reduced before meaningful dialogue can begin. The road to a solution is not helped by increasing a military presence.' Meanwhile our reporter David McFarlane has been putting together today's events so far in this rapidly developing story."

"It certainly is Helen. It is becoming increasingly difficult to keep up with events, not helped by a lack of information from the UK Government. Security at Faslane Naval Base where the Trident nuclear submarines are serviced has been replaced by crack SBS commandos under the direct authority of the Ministry of Defence. Yet another signal from the Westminster Government position on Scotland's independence couldn't be clearer with a warning to the Royal Scots Dragoon Guards to remain in their barracks. What would happen if they chose to ignore the warning is unclear. Barbed wire and barricades are being erected around Holyrood with soldiers from England refusing entry. Similar restrictions are taking place at St Andrews House in Edinburgh, government offices at Victoria Quay in Leith and Atlantic Quay in Glasgow. This has effectively ended all Scottish Government and Scottish civil service administration. Local authority powers have so far not been affected. We understand that staff at STV and BBC's headquarters at Pacific Quay have been ordered to leave and premises are being sealed. A statement from the Scottish Government has warned Westminster that the 'draconian' tactics will not frighten or intimidate the Scottish people and significantly that a 24 hour national strike is planned and will be called without further warning. It has urged all taxes previously due to the Treasury to be withheld. This will be the biggest peaceful civil disobedience protest that the British Isles have ever seen and she gave this warning. This from the First Minister."

"If Westminster continues to invade and occupy Scotland there will be serious repercussions that will be felt in London. I urge Prime Minister Keating to pull back from the brink of a disastrous policy in Scotland before it is too late. There is a limit to the patience that the Scottish People will endure in the face of highly provocative actions. We have sought a peaceful solution but our attempts to bring sense to Westminster have fallen on deaf ears. Westminster will simply not accept the wishes of the Scottish people for an independent Scotland. The message is clear, you can have democracy as long as it's the right kind of democracy. The truth is democracy is dead but we will prevail."

David McFarlane appeared again in the studio against a still image of crowds being dispersed with tear gas and the words 'Scotland in Crisis' in lurid red below.

"I've been talking to some insiders within the Scottish government and there are genuine fears that a concerted guerrilla campaign focussed not in Scotland but in England could begin. The tension amongst senior officials is visible. There is the feeling now that anything can happen and they say that the remarkable thing is that violence has not already taken to the streets."

14

'I'm worried about you, hearing that things are getting out of hand, come to Stavanger please. Love you xx'

Iona smiled and began replying to the text when the doorbell rang. "Where the hell have you been?"

Llewellyn had a sheepish grin. "I couldn't stick around here all day I went to the zoo, it was great. Have you been? The Meerkats are stars. Can't remember the last time I went to a zoo, why what's wrong."

"You're supposed to be dead."

"Were you worried about me?"

Iona snorted. "Don't flatter yourself."

She replied to Bjørge then clicked on her mobile video scrolling through the files until she saw Bjørge, eating, drinking, being silly, talking to the kilted Scotsman with the long beard on the flight to Scotland and then the video from the bus.

"What's that?" Emlyn caught a glimpse peering over her shoulder, "is that your boyfriend?"

"No, I was almost caught up in a riot."

"Let's see." He took the phone from her as the bald man appeared from the tourist shop stared after the two youths and turned towards Princess Street. Emlyn reversed the video and paused it.

"I know this guy."

"What?"

"I know him, well I think I do, I mean I don't know his name but he's familiar. There's something about that look. I've seen it before. I can't remember where. You know when you go into a shop on the high street regularly and you know the shop assistant and the next time you see her in a different context away from the shop the face is familiar but you can't remember how or where?" Iona looked puzzled, Emlyn laughed. "No, he doesn't work in a shop but I'm pretty sure he's from London. Sorry I can't think where about though," he said handing her phone back. "Look what am I doing here I can't stay dead for ever."

"How old are you?"

"Twenty-three, why?"

"You look seventeen. I've been talking to my supervisor. You could work for us."

"I don't want to be a double agent."

"Why not? You're Welsh."

"What's that got to do with it and I've got this overwhelming desire to stay alive."

"How about you work for us in Scotland. We'll give you a new identity, a proper one."

"What about my family and friends? I'll never see them again."

"So what do you propose, walking into Jane Caddish's office and saying hi Jane I'm back?"

"Amnesia?"

"I've been thinking about that. I don't think they'd buy it you might end up being water-boarded."

"How about you and I going off somewhere together until all this blows over, you know somewhere like Portugal or Ireland or Lanzarote?"

Iona looked at him with a mixture of incredulity and disbelief. He was not at all like Bjørge although his slightly scruffy beard and long hair made him look more Scandinavian than her boyfriend. There was a touching almost childlike innocence about the question. She smiled and shook her head. There was something about him that she was drawn to, like a lost puppy waiting for affection. Perhaps it was the mother in her. He was undoubtedly hapless and hopeless, clearly someone who had always lived at home tied to his mother's apron strings.

"I've told you Emlyn there's no you and me. You don't know much about women do you?"

"I know that you like me and I like you, what else is there to know."

"Much, much more."

"I got you a present," he said reaching into his rucksack.

It was in a plastic bag with Edinburgh Zoo written on the side. He handed it to her awkwardly. Iona opened it looked in and smiled.

"What's this?" she asked.

"It's a chameleon. Look," he said taking it from her. "The eyes move independently see? And the tongue unfurls and springs back, isn't that great.

It even has a prehensile tail that can cling on to anything. I remembered a reference in the file about your liking for chameleons."

Iona looked puzzled. "You're nuts, in a nice way. I don't know about Chameleon, Chamomile maybe."

"What's that?"

"Tea."

"Tea? Why would they want to know your taste in tea?"

"They like to keep us happy at GCHQ, it was my request. Anyway it was a very nice thought, thank you."

She kissed him on the cheek and he blushed.

Crowds in George Square and Princess Street Gardens gathered hours before the curfew to hear political and trade union leaders speak. Journalists, photographers and film crews were informed that there would be no exemptions to curfew including the media. Armed soldiers stayed in the background in Glasgow as riot and mounted police attempted to block off Cochrane Street, Queen Street and St Vincent Place in an attempt to encircle the crowd. A newly acquired water cannon parked outside Queen Street Station was surrounded by protesters waving placards. Speaker after speaker implored the crowd to remain peaceful and promised that passive civil disobedience would work in time. It was nearing seven when the loudspeakers started warning the protesters about the curfew. Normally attired police were not in evidence. Usually they would be there to persuade protesters to disperse. Edinburgh's Princess Street Garden gates had been locked but someone had opened them allowing over a hundred thousand protestors to enter. Speakers patiently queued at the wings of the Ross Band Stand while others held the crowd in passionate speeches that brought cheers and clapping. Several military helicopters continuously circled with searchlights provocatively strafing the crowd. 7.0pm and the warnings began over loudspeakers.

"The curfew has begun please return to your homes. This is an illegal gathering please return to your homes. You will be arrested if you do not disperse and return to your homes."

In Glasgow the snatch squads arrived targeting the speakers and bundling them with tie wrapped wrists into waiting vans. As a consequence scuffles broke out and the water cannon moved menacingly closer. Mounted police tried to break up the crowd by attempting to push them aside but they simply regrouped. Batons were draw by the riot police and banged aggressively against their riot shields.

In Edinburgh the acting First Minister was giving an impassioned plea for calm amidst the provocation. "The end result of violent action is that many people will get hurt and I do not want to see that I do not want to be any part of that. We have a democratically elected Government with a democratic mandate for self-determination and we will achieve this peacefully. As Mahatma Gandhi once said, *'Non-violence is the greatest force at the disposal of mankind.'* He achieved his goal and set India free. He also said, *'First they ignore you, then they laugh at you, then they fight you, then you win.'*

Snatch squads raced forward and arrested acting First Minister Constance Black and other speakers, taking them away. The crowd jeered the riot police and then there was silence, a strange silence in the presence of so many people. All that could be heard was the chatter of the helicopter rotor blades high above and then threats over the loudspeakers but the crowd and the silence remained. One woman sat down followed by another and another until everyone was sitting arms folded cross legged. The warnings continued. Tear gas was fired but the crowd buried their faces into their coats and jackets and remained. More threats of severe actions if they did not disperse rained down on them to no avail. Mounted police tried to get into the crowd but they were so tightly packed it was impossible. Then a very strange thing happened. Lightning lit up the gardens followed by a sonorous metallic roll of thunder. The air was very still. The sound of the helicopters faded as they left one by one leaving everyone looking up in anticipation of something. A late autumnal light shower of hailstones drifted downwards at first, becoming heavier as bigger hailstones hammered the ground covering everyone and everything with a coating of white. The woman who had sat down first lifted her phone and switched on the light, others followed. It was a triumph of passive protesting. A hundred thousand people holding aloft their lit mobiles swaying from side to side and then a song started by the same woman that caught and ran like wildfire through the white waving torch-lit crowd with the haunting words of a familiar chorus.

'Ah but let me tell you that I love you...and I think about you all the time,
Caledonia you're calling me and now I'm going home,
But if I should become a stranger you know that it would make me more than
sad,
Caledonia's been everything I've ever had.'

The dying echoes of the immortal lyrics written by Dougie Maclean caused many a tear as the song faded to silence. Everyone slowly stood up applauded then left.

At 3.50am four motorbike riders accompanying four, six axle drawbar trucks, trundled towards the M25's Bell Common tunnel from opposite directions. One entered and stopped halfway along the tunnel while the other blocked the entrance. The pattern was repeated on the other carriageway. The motorcyclists stopped and picked up the drivers and left satisfied that there was nobody in the tunnel. Shortly after forty tons of explosives on each truck detonated causing both tunnels to collapse. The trucks blocking the entrance took most of the blast shielding some early commuters waiting for the police to arrive and clear the motorway. The result was the end of a crucial arterial route circling London.

Constance Black was led from a police cell and taken to an interview room where four men with grim faces were waiting. "We have just received reports that the Bell Common tunnel has been blown up, is this your doing?"

"I have no knowledge of this, I did not order it."

"So much for peaceful protests."

"Was anyone hurt?"

"Never mind that who authorised this."

"As much as I would like the idea I do not control people's thoughts or minds. I have always said violence of any kind is unacceptable, sadly violence breeds violence gentlemen as you see. Has anyone claimed responsibility?"

"No."

"Have you heard of the term *agent provocateurs*? Because I believe that this invasion of Scotland was precipitated by them and for all I know possibly this tunnel. It seems to me to be a strange target where is it?"

"It is part of the M25 and carries, used to carry a great deal of traffic. There will now be a huge amount of chaos on the roads around and leading into London."

"Well I'm assuming that since you didn't answer my question nobody got hurt. I am not in charge of anything least of all planning or authorising insurgency operations. I do not have a parliament or a government I have no powers over Police Scotland all of these are now controlled by Number 10. You realize that no good will arise from the heavy handed illegal tactics of the British Prime Minister. Scotland has changed and there will be no going back whatever institutions are dismantled. If and I say with a big emphasis on the if, the tunnel explosion was committed by someone from Scotland, someone out with my control, I would hazard a guess that this could be the very beginning of a protracted guerrilla war and this is merely a warning shot across the bows. That's a personal view of course."

"There's no Scottish news on the radio or the internet." Emlyn was mulling over some porridge.

"Or television, there's been a news blackout after last night but the buzz is that almost all of the government have been arrested along with trade union leaders. Even the unionist political parties in Scotland are getting angry about the shutdown of government. If anything it could antagonise large sections of the no camp leaving the diehards."

"Is it all about work with you?" The uncharacteristic question surprised Iona. "You don't talk about anything personal, yourself, your dog, your family, your friends you don't even talk about your boyfriend what's his name?"

"It's Bjørge and I don't have a dog."

Iona stood up and ran through to the bathroom to be sick. She returned to the kitchen and began nibbling her Marmite on toast distracted by what he had said. Was she really that introspective, married to her job like Jane. That would never do.

"Anyway what do you mean?"

"Well when you talk to what's his name what do you two talk about?"

"I'm not telling you that, it's private."

"See?"

Iona sighed, a little irritated. "We talk about all kinds of things, politics, religion, art, cooking, music, everything."

Emlyn looked at her vacantly. "Sport?"

"No not sport, look I'm going to head off shortly..."

"...Iona," he said softly.

She looked at him. He didn't say her name like that very often.

"Our destiny is entwined. Somehow we have been thrown together by fate you and me, for some weird purpose. You need me as much as I need you. We're in this together, to what end? I don't know. You don't understand, I have lived my life so far with a plan of sorts, something that I can cling on to knowing where I might be going and that when all the uncertainties of life are thrown at you I would at least have a plan to fall back on, do you see. Now I'm in a vacuum. I have no idea what I am doing here or where I'm going."

Iona hugged him and she pulled away as he kissed her neck. She let go and picked up her phone.

"Grace its Iona I want to bring Emlyn in."

15

"What happened to you?"

"Nothing important."

Capello's cheek looked bruised and swollen. He took out a handkerchief and spat some blood onto it wiping his mouth. The pain of extracting the tooth himself was preferable to going to the dentist. No whisky no painkillers just the neat sharp pliers of a Leather-man, a short countdown from three, two, one, a twist and pull, all over.

Jane looked on in disgust. 'What a strange man this was,' she thought, 'it was just as well he was good at what he did.' "You might need some antibiotics."

"I don't touch drugs."

Jane shrugged her shoulders and gazed out the window.

"Sir Cyrus Steele said you had a job for me," he said.

She watched the puffy white clouds race by carried on an autumnal wind. When she was inside she sometimes felt claustrophobic and wanted to escape but when she was outside she felt vulnerable, unsure and overly cautious about everything. All she needed was right here, canteens of different quality depending on status, exercise and game rooms even night rooms that were mostly used in emergencies. There was no need to leave apart from having contact with ordinary people, people with normal lives and doing normal things like shopping or cooking in her empty flat. She turned her chair and looked at him.

"The Scottish government such as it is has deployed a company called Softwarehouse to process and analyse Intel. They're communicating via an encrypted satellite connection so we don't know where they are but what we do know is that they are busy little bees and someone there has been targeting our servers. We are changing encryption keys but not quickly enough and added to that everyone in my department is working twenty-four hours a day trying to find the Bell Common bombers. Sir Cyrus want you to go back to Edinburgh and find the department head to carry out an executive action. This is not much but it's all we've got on her," she said passing the folder.

Capello opened it. There was just a ten by eight matt photograph with a typed paper caption cow-gummed onto the back.

"Grace Ross-Quinn, Is that it?"

"That's it. We've tried face recognition with no result. Put her and Softwarehouse out of business permanently. Perhaps a fire would cause maximum disruption. There is one other thing before you do that. He wants you to go to Stirling. I believe there is going to be a huge demonstration. It has been suggested that you find a rooftop and shoot three or four riot police, injuries no deaths. That should get the party going."

Capello tried to stop pushing his tongue into the hole left by the missing tooth. "This is the last time Jane. I think it's time for me to quit."

She looked at Oriel Capello and nodded. "How will you live? Do you still have family in Catalan?"

"No. Most of my family have emigrated and I've lost touch with those still there. I've been putting aside some money, might try growing olives, not in Catalan though, maybe Italy or Portugal." Capello smiled and stood up, he had no intention of olive farming anywhere.

"Well you know your identity is closely guarded so you won't need a new one. But if you do want a new ID we can arrange that. And of course Oriel if anything goes wrong we don't know you, understand?" he smiled again leaned forward and shook her outstretched hand.

'...her lips were moist and inviting. He took her hand and squeezed.

"My ship leaves for Antigua on the high tide at six bells."

"Take this locket with a strand of my hair lest you forget." She said closing her eyes, her heart racing.

"Forget? How could I ever forget my dear? You will be with me on my journey. You will be with me always."

A waft of salt laden sea air through the open window caused the candles to splutter dimming the room as they kissed...'

The hand that held the book relaxed letting it slip gently onto the duvet as the pages fluttered together. Iona's eyes closed.

Iona woke with the sound of a low flying helicopter circling above. For a full minute she had no idea where she was. Then she remembered. Just as the helicopter sounds faded she got a kick from a tiny foot in her abdomen and gasped. Then a wave of emotion and elation followed. She wished Bjørge was in bed with her to share the moment. Her door opened.

"Are you ok the helicopter woke me up and I heard a noise?"

Emlyn came in and sat on the edge of the bed looking concerned. He brushed the sleep from his eyes. Iona folded down the duvet lifted her t-shirt a little and took his hand placing in on her bare swollen tummy. She closed her eyes and the baby kicked again.

"My God," he said pulling his hand away momentarily in surprise then placed it back again. "That's fantastic."

He leaned forward and gently placed the side of his head to her tummy, listening. Iona's fingers touched his hair. She gasped again as the baby kicked once more.

"I think he's going to be footballer," she said.

"I can hear the heart beating, yes, no your heart of course and another. That's amazing."

"You saved two lives Em," she said pulling aside the duvet.

Emlyn raised his head and looked at her. She raised an eyebrow. He climbed in and covered them both as she turned away from him. She took his arm and drew it across her tummy smiling to herself. Emlyn relaxed. He could feel the baby move again. Somehow being in bed with Iona seemed perfectly natural. He gently kissed the back of her neck.

"Iona I can't stop thinking about you," he whispered. "I think you're gorgeous. I like everything about you even although I know you love Bjørge. I love the way your nose wrinkles when you laugh and sometimes you chew the inside of your lip without realizing it. And when you take your contact lenses out your eyes go a bit funny until you put your glasses on. We are the same you and me working in the intelligence community and we think alike. Remember that time I was saying something and you said you were having the same thought. I wrote a poem for you. It's maybe corny but it's how I feel about us. Iona I love you...Iona?"

Emlyn could hear gentle snoring. He turned on his back and stared at the ceiling allowing memories to flood in.

"What is true? That which can be verified? Cross-checked? Supported by evidence? Perhaps, but verification is dependent on the quality of the verifier. Cross-checking can throw up confusing anomalies. Evidence can be tainted and at the end of the day a high statistical probability of reality is the best we can ever do but it is still...*infinitely* superior to perceptions. What we perceive to be true is where we begin, not where we end. Some of you may have a James Bond perception of the way we work at SIS. That is not what we do. I don't believe anyone here has worked in the city but there are similarities in the way information is processed, the main difference being the type of information that comes across our desks. The digital era has changed forever the way we exchange information and it's fast. Specially formulated logarithms can sift through vast amounts of information processed by next generation computing almost in real time. This gives us a head start against terrorists, and cyber warriors. Make no mistake there is a cyber-war that is escalating exponentially right now. Groups sanctioned and supported by foreign powers are developing methods of attacking our infrastructure as I speak. The general public are largely unaware that defence, energy, transport and the corporate sector are being targeted daily. But we still need people in the field and that's why you are here. Now this course is not long enough so there is a lot to pack in over the next few weeks. Good luck everyone."

That is how it all started. Emlyn could remember every single word the instructor said and precisely how he felt at the time. Nervous, excited, apprehensive and eager to learn soaking it all up, imbibing the detail in great gulps like a dehydrated animal at a lush watering hole, until his intellectual thirst was slaked. They were heady times indeed and now he was here in bed with a woman he hardly knew. A woman he loved who didn't love him and in a strange way it didn't seem to matter. He could make her love him...if he knew how.

"Thank you," said Iona ladling out the porridge.

"What for?"

"Last night."

"I didn't do anything."

"That's what I mean, but you were there when I really needed someone. I was feeling a bit vulnerable and you could have taken advantage of me and didn't."

"I'm not gay."

"I know that," she said.

"Did you hear anything I said last night?"

"I don't think so, go on."

"No, another time."

"We're going to have to find somewhere else to live it's not fair on Dottie, if they still think we're dead maybe it would be ok if we went home."

"Home?"

"Mum's house."

"Are you going to tell Bjørge?" asked Emlyn.

"What about?"

"Last night of course."

"What's to tell?"

"You slept with a strange man."

"No, he can get terribly jealous." Iona put some single cream on her porridge. "I don't mind him being a little jealous I take it as a sign of his undying love for me but he would most likely kill you, it's the Viking blood in him," Emlyn went white. "He would do it in unorthodox way of course, he's very inventive. I heard him mulling over the idea once of gaffer taping someone to the blade of a wind turbine. I would imagine the brain would be mince in a gale."

"That's not funny."

Iona laughed. The latch clicked on the front door allowing traffic noise to enter and seconds later Dottie came in.

"Hi Dottie, I was just saying...are you alright?"

Dottie sat down at the kitchen table and started crying. Emlyn felt awkward and embarrassed while Iona got up to hug her.

"I'm sorry, I'm exhausted," she said. "People are still breaking the curfew and being arrested. By the time I see them there are broken ribs and concussion. Some have respiratory problems with CS gas, injuries with pepper sprays, rubber bullets and Tasers, we're overrun at A&E. I was told to go home by the consultant."

"I made some porridge Dottie."

"I don't even have the energy to eat."

Iona took her coat off and began massaging her shoulders while Emlyn ladled out the porridge and added milk.

"You have to have something to eat and then off to bed," Iona said.

"There are an increasing number of younger people, even school kids coming in, it's like a war zone." She put her hand across her head and looked up. "Thanks Iona I feel better already. You two look a bit flushed is it too hot in here?"

"No it's fine. Dottie I think we'll have to split. We've been here quite a long time, it was only meant to be a couple of days."

"Don't be silly I like having you both around, stay as long as you want. Anyway I'm hardly ever here. I might have to travel to the Forth Valley."

"Where?"

"Forth Valley Royal Hospital it's in in Larbert."

"Why?" asked Emlyn.

"Don't you know? There's going to be a massive demonstration over the weekend with people travelling from Aberdeen, Dundee, Edinburgh and Glasgow converging at Stirling. The police say there could be upward of a million and half people going to be there over the weekend so another curfew battle but this time it could get really serious. It's not just us, a number of hospitals are drafting in staff."

"We'd better get into the office," said Iona.

Jenny Leask was on automatic. The 'how are you today?' greeting was probably in the mid-hundreds and there was still another two hours to go before she finished her shift in Lidl's supermarket. It had felt like a very long day. She sensed the beginning of cramp on the back of her leg and shifted her weight on the stool. Cornflakes, rice, bread, eggs, potatoes, milk, crisps and so on pinging their way past.

"Now that'll be eighteen pounds and thirty-three pence please," she said with the obligatory smile. "That's a twenty and one pound sixty-seven change, thank you."

She waited while the man with the tweed jacket and bonnet filled his shopping bag and left before standing up and stretching. A pallet of tinned vegetables was waiting to be stacked on depleted shelves. She sighed and started the task when there was a light touch on her shoulder.

"Hi Jenny have you got a minute."

"I told you Graeme the boss knows you and she won't like it."

"I know, I know it'll just take a second."

"It was a minute a second ago."

Graeme smiled. "I've got a job for you at the weekend a gig in Stirling, there's going to be hundreds of thousands of people, it'll be worthwhile."

Graeme was a hard working caterer who always saw the possibility of an opportunity.

"The hamburger van's been done up, it's a lot better now and Sheila and Pat are serving as well."

"I don't know. I was thinking about going through to Glasgow to see my boyfriend."

"Tell him to come through it's a two day gig I've booked accommodation. It'll be fun and," he rubbed his fingers together, "lots of moolah."

"Ok. Now go before I get into trouble my supervisor is probably watching us on the security cameras."

16

"So Emlyn, I believe we have a lot to thank you for."

Grace was eating a Danish pastry with bits flying out of her mouth and at the same time as the words came tumbling out so did the crumbs landing on her voluminous vibrant blue dress. She brushed them away without looking or seeming to care. Her short stubby hands were adorned with dark blue nail varnish and displayed on the index finger of the right hand, a gold ring with an enamelled Lapis Lazuli forget-me-not. She was wearing a silver necklace entwining twelve polished oval Blue-John stones and matching earrings.

"It was nothing," he said with false modestly, slightly embarrassed to be the focus of attention.

Grace stopped eating and carefully touched both corners of her mouth with a linen hankie that had a G in Harrington font, sewn on. She picked up a plain white mug and took a sip fixing him with her eyes.

"On the contrary Emlyn, Iona is a very valuable member of our little community now."

"No, I didn't mean that. It was just luck that I was there in time and..." he tailed off as she interjected.

"Anyway I believe you want to work for us, is that right?"

"Yes, of course," he shrugged, "events conspire."

"They certainly do my boy, they certainly do." Grace looked at them both and put her hands together. "Now, is there anything I should know?"

Emlyn looked at Iona and blushed.

"No," said Iona holding Grace's gaze."

"Excellent. I want you two to go to Stirling. We have face recognition up and running. If we could prove that the PM is orchestrating a group within Scotland it would blow apart their rhetoric. So Emlyn I want you to film the group opposing the demonstration. Iona you will scan Emlyn's images to identify who these people are and congratulations by the way. When's the baby due?"

"Oh thanks Grace somewhere near the end of February. He's kicking," Iona beamed. "I wonder if I could check someone out, I have a video clip on my phone would it be possible to test the face recognition software?"

"Of course who is it?"

"It was during the demonstration on George Street. I saw two youths rushing from a tourist shop and then a man came out after they had fled. There was something about him, an assuredness like someone who knows how to look after himself, I may be completely wrong."

"Worth a try. Emlyn you're from a Celtic nation like us and you might not realize it but that matters."

"Never really given it much thought."

"Not fancy home rule for Wales?"

Emlyn left the question unanswered. He had briefly considered it and, given different circumstances he might have wanted Wales to be independent. As it was, a greater say in the running of the country wouldn't go amiss. His father was a staunch Labour councillor through and through and feared nationalism in any form. There were too many *ists and ites,* for his liking conveniently used as shorthand for lazy journo's. Communists, fascists, nationalists, separatists, Blairites, Brownites the list was depressingly endless. It would be fair to say that it left Emlyn apolitical, not for any high moral standpoint though he had read about conflicts of interest and MP's expenses etc. No, he just didn't care.

"I don't know," he said eventually.

"Ok pick up a comms van from the depot you know your way round one of these?" he nodded. Grace turned to her monitor. "Iona's familiar with it as well, Ok scoot."

Emlyn went to the store and picked a camera that he was vaguely familiar with and returned to Iona's desk. He was reading the manual when Iona started tutting.

"Nothing, absolutely nothing," she said annoyed. "James are you sure this face recognition software is operational?"

Her red haired neighbour nodded. "Works for me. You're pal can't be on the grid."

"I thought everyone was on the grid."

"There are groups that are not allowed on the grid, no social media, twitter, Facebook, Google, nothing."

"Who?"

"People like you and me and Psyops, black-ops, field agents and of course the paranoid are never on the grid."

"Could just be a red herring, curious though no digital activity? Damn it, I hate when a lead goes cold like this. If only I could just rule him out."

"I'm pretty sure I've seen him around, can't remember where though, could be wrong."

"Emlyn you're not being helpful think harder."

He shook his head. "Nope."

"I've booked two single rooms in separate bed and breakfasts, basic security precautions nothing personal."

"Where about?"

"Bridge of Allan. I take it you can drive?" she asked.

"I hope so, I have the comms van."

"I'm sorry m'dear your room's gone." The guest house owner Mrs Patchett looked harassed and embarrassed. "My daughter let it out without telling me."

Emlyn looked around the B&B hall for inspiration. A fussy Edwardian ebonised hall table had a matching mirror frame above. Six flying Beswick mallards adorned flower patterned wallpaper, three at either side of the mirror. Below, two nineteen fifties oak hall chairs at either side of the table, completed the attempt at a link with history. Next to the glazed dining room door was a genuine Georgian, long case clock accompanied by an incongruous three foot cardboard waiter on a stand wearing a red tail coat and holding a menu card. It had been a tiring journey with all the one way traffic, the congestion, streams of people walking, cycling and hitch-hiking, now he was standing in a B&B hallway in the Bridge of Allan with the breakfast's bacon smell still evident, wafting from the kitchen and being told his room had gone.

"That's disappointing," he said thinking what else could he say?

"If you're really stuck we've got an old caravan in the garden, but it's being used as a hen house at the moment we could clean it up though."

"I'm allergic to feathers," he lied, "thanks anyway."

He closed the mock Georgian white painted door and walked down the narrow gravel path back to the van where Iona was waiting. She looked up as he got in the van.

"Mrs Patchett daughter let my room," he said closing the door and starting the engine. "It's an adventure, deal with it," he said to nobody in particular.

Iona was busy texting. He managed to turn into a main street but the traffic soon ground to a halt. It wasn't far to the other guest house but today it would seem far enough. He switched the radio on. It was one of those interminable call-in shows. Inarticulate people on crackly mobiles with good arguments, were constantly being interrupted by the studio presenter, while articulate perfect audio studio 'experts', were left in peace to postulate preposterous viewpoints in the name of balance. He looked across at Iona. She was uncharacteristically chewing gum.

"What," she said.

"Nothing," he looked away then back, "you're chewing gum."

"So," she turned up her nose and blew a huge bubble which burst on her phone. "Look what you made me do," she shrieked slapping him on the shoulder.

Emlyn laughed as she spat on a paper hanky and feverishly attempted to wipe off the sticky gum. Eventually they got moving and after what seemed an age, arrived at the Rose-Lee Guest House. It was a large detached Edwardian pile with its own pink granite gravel drive. The guest house had been a partnership between Rose and her husband Lee who had passed away unexpectedly at a relatively early age some years before. This time, the hall had a bit of class. The pitch pine floorboards had been sanded and varnished to high gloss. Not one but two longcase clocks were at either side of the door. One was a mid-Georgian mahogany clock with a silvered brass chapter ring and a ship that rocked in time. An antique Afghan Baluch runner laid out along the hallway. An Edwardian sofa with original covering in a busy flowery pattern had pink cushions on it. There were several Georgian and Victorian tables with Satsuma and Famille Verte vases, filled with fresh cut flowers that gave off a lovely scent. A door opened.

Rose Patterson, "please call me Rose," was an attractive late forties gregarious women who enjoyed people. She was confident and capable with a firm handshake, very much in charge of her domain. She had been washing pans in the kitchen and had dried her hands on a pinafore that said 'Too many cooks welcome, I hate broth.'

"There are two of you, I was expecting one. No matter it's a double bed if that's all right. I'm sure it will be," she winked. "Now you must be Iona, what a lovely name, have you been there? It's a wonderful island with lovely beaches, and you are?

"Emlyn."

"Emelyn? That's an unusual name for a boy."

"No Emlyn, I'm from Wales."

"Oh you're having a baby Iona that's wonderful, congratulations to the pair of you, when's the baby due?"

"Thanks, it's the end of February but..."

"...Is it your first, I remember my first it was so exciting and scary at the same time. Do you know the sex? I had a boy I knew all along it would be, even bought the clothes beforehand, Lee thought I was daft. Let me show you your room."

She led the way up stairs before they could answer. On the half landing attached to the wall was a Viennese wall clock with a swinging polished brass pendulum. Made of oak, it had an arched top with a dental cornice and a beautifully engraved dial. The bedroom was pleasantly decorated in a minimalist way with a plain oatmeal carpet and cream painted walls with a couple of scenic prints of the cairngorms. On either side of the large double bed were modern side cabinets with late famille jaune porcelain based lamps. On the bed was a tartan throw covering the duvet. The spacious room held a wall length mirror sliding door into a fitted wardrobe and to the right, behind an opaque glass door, was an en-suite, all white bathroom. The large bay window with folded pitch pine shutters commanded a magnificent view of the Ochils.

"I hope you're not up for the weekend demonstration Iona especially in your condition, Lord knows what's going to happen. You should have a walk up the Ochils it's wonderful up there Lee and I used to go every weekend without fail," she sighed. "Now there's the key and if there's anything you need just give me a shout."

"Rose," Iona said gently, "Emlyn is a colleague of mine, he is not my partner and his room was let out by mistake, you wouldn't happen to have another bedroom."

"I'm so sorry dear we're completely full, everywhere is." She looked at Emlyn mischievously.

"I have a king-size and I don't mind sharing," she said smiling.

Iona looked at him and stifled a grin as he turned red. "That's very kind of you Rose," he said. "It's only a couple of nights I'm sure I'll find somewhere. I wouldn't want to take advantage of you. I mean of your hospitality."

"You can take advantage of my hospitality any time you like."

Iona smiled. "Thanks Rose we'll work something out."

Rose gave him a lingering flirtatious smile and left the two of them alone.

"You missed a trick there Em," she said, "Wealthy widow, attractive, with a good business, walks in the Ochils."

"Thanks," He said drily, "she's probably old enough to be my mother any way never mind that, you're in denial."

"Exactly what am I denying?"

"You don't get it, you and me are destined to be together, really it's written in the stars, don't you think? I'm Scorpio what are you?"

A pained look crossed her face. "I'm not telling you."

"Ha," he said. "You're Scorpio too."

"You've seen my file and anyway I don't believe you."

"I have seen your file," He said slowly. "But I am, so you see...."

Her pained look was replaced by a comically stern expression on her face.

"...I'll sleep in the van," he said. Iona wrinkled her nose and smiled. She knew she was going to have to give in. She wouldn't have been able to sleep knowing he was in the van.

17

Iona felt hot and uncomfortable, she wasn't sure if the heating was on or not. Maybe it was because Emlyn was in bed with her yet again, albeit at the other side of a bolster made with spare pillows. Maybe it was the baby. She was on her side with an extra pillow between her legs to take the pressure off. Going to the toilet more frequently now didn't help. He was snoring. Not the raucous full blown toadesque snoring that big macho men do it was more gentile, rhythmic and soothing like soft breaking waves. She felt unaccountably happy, lying in bed for the second time really with *almost* a complete stranger. Were there feelings for Em lurking in her subconscious? She brushed that aside. There had never been secrets between her and Bjørge, well not secrets that matter. Should she tell him? What would he think? What would he say? These were strange times. She very carefully got out of bed so as not to wake him and checked the radiator, it was off.

She walked across to the window and found that her walk had changed to accommodate the extra weight. The catch on the window opened quietly letting in a welcome breeze. Emlyn turned over and the snoring stopped. She could just go to Norway and leave all these complications but the calling was too strong. It was more than just a job it was about the future, her future and her baby's future. There was another kick from inside and it made her feel emotional. There was a living new person inside her waiting to get out into the world, one of natures' miracles. God she could do with a drink. She felt her breasts. They were definitely getting bigger and sagging a little. She was putting on weight and occasionally getting out of breath. She looked outside. It was a street with imposing houses that would have been filled with professors and lecturers, merchant bankers and well to do antique dealers that had moved on.

Now it was a street of guest houses bed and breakfasts and conversions into flats. A light came on in the upstairs room of the house opposite. A woman with a baby pacing back and fore, maybe the baby couldn't sleep or teething, windy, hungry or needing a nappy change. That's what the future held, so what was her baby's future? How was it that she had become inextricably linked to this Welshman as if there was an invisible umbilical cord? She had come to respect him and his innocence. He had a sense of morality and honour that was rare in men. She wondered how Bjørge would have behaved under similar circumstances, no, let's not go there. She needed something, something to eat or drink and she didn't know what.

Maybe she should go downstairs and investigate the fridge. She felt guilty about not keeping in touch with her mother and Bjørge, why was that? She looked over at Emlyn. This was crazy. She held up her left hand and rubbed her empty ring finger. That would change she thought. He turned over facing her. He was quite good looking in an odd sort of way. She sighed. Would it do any harm, just the once, she couldn't get pregnant after all, she already was. What Bjørge didn't know wouldn't harm him. She made towards the bed. He looked so innocent. She bit her lip and touched the duvet. Her phone on the bedside table vibrated making her jump. She picked it up looked at it then hurried into the bathroom and sat on the toilet seat lid.

"Hey I hope I didn't wake you up."

"Hello you it's so nice to hear your voice. You didn't waken me I couldn't sleep. I was just thinking of you actually."

"You sound funny where are you?"

"Oh in the bathroom."

"Bathroom? Why?"

"Don't be silly."

"I have to see you."

"Is there something wrong?"

"No I'm missing you terribly. I've got a few days off and I'm coming to Scotland."

"You can't."

"Why? Is everything ok? I was getting worried because you hadn't phoned."

"Everything is fine, there's a lot of stuff happening and I've been really busy. Bjørge You can't come over just now, I'm not in Edinburgh. I'm sorry I can't explain. In a few days' time I should be clear. I'll call. Oh the baby's started kicking."

"Really, I wish I could be with you."

"I think he's going to be a footballer. I've stopped being sick in the mornings but I still get these cravings driving me nuts. I'll have to go. I'll call you, promise."

"Bye, love you."

"Love you too."

Iona looked at herself in the mirror and stroked her rounded tummy. She smiled as the baby moved slightly. She opened the door, switched off the light and closed it gently, her eyes adjusting to the dark.

Emlyn raised his head from the pillow. "I heard you talking."

"Bjørge called."

"Are you ok?" Emlyn was looking concerned.

"No I need some pickled onions and ice cream." Iona got into bed and sat resting her back against the headboard. "I'll just have to wait. Tell me something have you been through the Foundation Investigative Training course?"

"What's that?"

"Ok. What about the Intelligence Officer Development Programme?"

"Yes well not all of it, I did nine months...actually just over eight months."

"This is crazy. There is definitely something missing here. I know Jane Caddish, she's not stupid and she doesn't make mistakes. There must have been someone else watching you. Why would she do that? What would be the point of sending two agents separately if they were essentially doing the same job?"

"Because they're not doing the same job?" he said.

Iona thought for a minute and then it dawned on her. "Oh no," she put her hands to her face. "It couldn't be. Surely not. That bald headed man, he's from the Increment. You're a genius Emlyn and you don't know it."

"What's the increment?"

"It's a group of seriously bad guys, unofficial contract killers. It's a politically deniable group made up of ex SAS black ops killers. They carry out 'executive actions' or assassinations primarily for MI6 having been trained by Kidon an Israeli team of assassins. I never thought in a million years Jane would do anything like that. What on earth does she think I've got? Ok if that's the case he was tracking your phone and then after your text he would have known you had found me and would also have known where we were. I wonder if he was responsible for the bomb. No, impossible he couldn't have set it up in time. Logic dictates the reasoning that Jane and this mystery man thinks we're dead. I think I had a narrow escape."

"What'll we do?"

"We need to speak to Grace in the morning."

Capello used an untraceable credit card when hiring the 1299 Ducati Panigale. He strapped on a specially fitted case and stowed away a small bag, put on the hired leather gloves and helmet and headed north through suburban London setting off car alarms as he passed by. He knew that at speeds in excess of 190 mph he could outrun a police helicopter if necessary. The red and black sculpted lines of the machine seemed more like a piece of modern design that would not be out of place exhibited at the Centre for Modern Italian Art. At the third stop for fuel he came back from the shop to see it surrounded by a crowd of bikers with their arms folded shaking their heads salivating. They applauded as he left. He crossed the border in record time heading for Glasgow. Soon he was approaching Stirling, negotiating the walkers, cyclists, coaches and cars and eventually pulled into a high rise car park in the centre of the town overlooking an area that was already seeing large crowds gathering.

"Good morning and welcome to the news channel with me Helen Butler. Crowds are already gathering in unprecedented numbers in Stirling for the demonstration protesting at the martial law imposed due to unrest and bombings in Scotland and the arrest of government ministers. There is expected to be well over a million people making their way to a city park. There have been numerous reports of police road blocks and delayed train journeys. Organisers have criticised Police Scotland, claiming that it is an attempt to frustrate those wishing to join the demonstration. A spokesman for Police Scotland has said that it is acting in interests of public safety. Fleets of helicopters are taking oil rig workers who have gone on a two day strike back to shore. A spokesman for the North Sea Oil Industry has said that almost all productions platforms in the UK sector have had to be shut down. There will be a further delay of a twenty-four hour start-up period once the staff returns on Monday. European Security Council members are sending observers to monitor the situation. Since all the leaders of the Scottish Government are being held in custody there appears to be no one in authority appealing for calm and the fears are that this could be a potentially explosive stand-off. With me in the studio is security expert Jason Mulholland. Jason what are the potential flashpoints and do you think the authorities are equipped to deal with such a massive gathering?"

"Firstly let me say as a neutral that something has got to give. The shifting tectonic plates of UK Government ideology colliding with the rock hard cultural solidity in Scotland could be extremely dangerous. It has a very ominous feel to it. Any attempt to disperse such a large gathering of people in one place historically has always met with disaster. There is a build-up of riot police and a large number of troops in full combat dress that gives a very worrying expectation that this is becoming an arena of possible conflict. I fear that many people could get hurt."

"Is there anything that can be done to avert conflict?"

"Well this demonstration is a spontaneous reaction to events and it is effectively leaderless since all the main players are locked up. So who do the authorities speak to, there is no-one. If the Westminster Government is seriously wanting to de-escalate tensions here, they should allow a peaceful protest to run its course engage in dialogue, if necessary through a third party to determine what Scotland's future is going to be. No 10 has found itself up a blind alley with nowhere to go and perhaps the UN should step in before it's too late."

"Jason we're hearing that a number of power workers at generating plants throughout Scotland are going to join the demonstration inevitably leading to blackouts."

"This is a serious escalation. When the infrastructure of a country starts to falter and in this case its electricity but it could so easily be gas or water, then the integrity of society starts to break down. All the things we take for granted are not there anymore."

"The situation is changing fast I'm hearing from my producer that Forth Valley Royal Hospital has drafted in Doctors and nurses from other hospitals obviously expecting casualties, worrying times. Thank you very much Jason Mulholland. Now I think we can go over to our roving reporter Bill Duncannon who is somewhere in the crowd, Bill."

"Yes Helen we are on the edge of the crowd however we are not being allowed to get any closer in fact all of the satellite vans are being kept at a distance. Overhead the helicopters you hear and there are six of them are all police and army helicopters. The Government has proclaimed a civilian no fly zone over Stirling so there are no television helicopters allowed. There is it has to be said a holiday atmosphere here with several pipe bands playing. There are hamburger vans and the fine early October weather has helped to swell the numbers. This could be the biggest gathering of people in Scotland ever."

"Has there been any sign of trouble?"

"None whatsoever it is very much a party almost a festival feel to it."

"Thank you for now Bill. Now joining me in the studio is the leader of Stirling Council Andrew Bressick..."

"...Gressick."

"Sorry, Andrew Gressick, have you ever seen anything like it?"

"Never and can I say right at the outset please I implore the police and army to maintain a respectful distance from the gathering so as not to inflame passions. This is a perfectly legal protest and the build-up of the numbers of security personnel could be seen as highly provocative. It's a nice day and there's a carnival atmosphere but make no mistake people are here for a purpose and that's to tell the world that Scotland has been effectively invaded by England with many public institutions dismantled, broadband access interfered with, curfews and so on. I really hope that the authorities do not attempt to enforce a curfew this evening because I can guarantee it will not work."

"What do you think can be done to reduce tensions?"

"In a word, dialogue. You cannot impose your will over almost six million people without severe consequences for everyone involved. There has to be agreement. The stupidest thing Westminster did was lock up the country's leaders, who are they going to talk to now? This is not just going to go away with a show of force, it could escalate and I do not want to see that either. The worst case scenario is, if there is an influx of arms and people willing to challenge martial law, it could go downhill very quickly indeed."

"Thank you Andrew Gressick got your name right that time."

The layout of the inside of the manned covert surveillance van was pretty standard. It had all the electronic wizardry needed for speedy communication and relaying digital images. Six monitors, four of them linked to hidden external cameras, a radio link to a roving camera and an upload link connected to servers in Edinburgh.

"Well I think we're sorted, everything seems to work," said Emlyn closing the lens cap and switching the camera off, "happy?"

Iona nodded. "Listen," she said tweaking the monitors, "don't take any chances, things could get very ugly here. Keep your distance from the opposite camp and use the long end of the lens, it will still be effective for face recognition."

Emlyn smiled. "Worried about me?"

"I need you I can't drive, remember? Where are you going to start?"

Emlyn pulled out a 300mm lens with a doubler to show Iona. "I'm going to choose a high position overlooking the park and I'll just scan the crowd with this baby. Is the link ok?"

She nodded. "Good hunting and Em, I did mean look after yourself."

Emlyn slid the door open and joined the crowd. He looked for a vantage point and spotted a flat roofed telecoms building. He walked inside through the glass panel doors and up to reception where a smiling woman greeted him.

"Hello can I help?"

"Is it ok if I take some shots from the roof?"

"I don't think that'll be a problem, hold on," she picked up the phone. "Hi it's Marilyn I've got someone at the desk who would like to go on the roof to take pictures...Ok thanks. If you take the lift to the top there's a flight of stairs and," she reached into a drawer. "There's the key. Don't fall off."

The door swung open revealing a gravelled roof with several satellite dishes and antennae. Emlyn chose a spot next to a cowling, raised the tripod legs to waist level Attached the 600mm lens to the camera and fixed the base of the heavy lens to the tripod head releasing the pan and tilt lock.

"Iona can you hear me? I hope you're getting these images."

"Yeah it's all fine Em."

"Exactly which groups am I looking for?"

"Anyone waving a Union Jack."

18

Capello had assembled the Remington Modular Sniper Rifle. He checked the scope carefully making sure it was at the correct setting. There was something comforting about holding it. It was almost an extension of himself. He scanned the crowd, the young families, children playing together, mum and dad having an ice cream, teenagers kicking a ball about. There was some testing with a microphone on a makeshift stage and then over to the right were the targets, the riot police leaning against vans. A glint of something caught his eye on a roof top two buildings away. He swung the rifle across and refocused the scope. He stopped breathing and stared.

"Llewellyn!"

It was just a whisper but he was shocked nevertheless. If he was alive as he clearly was, so was McCallum. First things first. He loaded the rifle readjusted the sight and searched for his target. Wondering who he would choose to be heroes. The rifle coughed and the mark, a large tough looking guy fell to the ground clutching his leg. Three shots later and more wounded riot police and there was pandemonium. Soldiers started firing in the air in panic causing a stampede. He scanned the park for the last time resting on a hamburger van. There was a woman inside the van staring at him.

"Don't look," he said. She was shouting something. Capello swore and slammed his hand down on the parapet. "Don't point. I wish you hadn't seen me," he whispered. His rifle coughed again and she collapsed falling out of view.

Capello calmly disassembled and packed away the Remington, snapping the case shut. He took a note of where Llewellyn was, still unaware of what had been going on. He took the stairs two at a time until he reached the Ducati and strapped the case to it. He fired up the motorbike and took it down to ground level parking it in a bay next to the exit. He strode over to the communications building still wearing his helmet while people were rushing past in panic. Marilyn was standing at the glass doors wondering what was going on when Capello came in.

"Can I help?"

"There's a friend of mine on the roof he forgot to take a lens."

"Up the lift then keep going up the stairs. What's happening out there?" but he was already in the lift.

Colin shouted in horror as Jenny fell to the floor of the van. He knew what had happened right away but others stood still rooted to the spot. He climbed into the van. She was lying on her back her pale green pinafore stained with blood. He picked her up, kicked the door open and carried her away towards arriving ambulances. The paramedics raced over and carried her to the vehicle checking her pulse. The door closed and the ambulance took off with sirens going. A calm professionalism took over. Colin went back to the hamburger van but it had already gone leaving behind the marks on the grass where it had been. He turned his back to where Jenny would have been standing and scanned the horizon. It could only have been a sniper's bullet, no sound and a single shot it had to be but where? On the right was a tall office block, to the left a smaller building and further over to the left a multi-storey car park. He looked at the angle of the building and remembering Jenny's position when she was hit that was the most likely place.

"Iona, soldiers have started firing at the crowd all hell is breaking loose everyone is panicking and running. I've lost my target group they've dispersed smartish."

"Hello Emlyn," Capello stood behind him holding a pistol by his side scanning the horizon then turned resting his gaze on the startled man.

"Em who's that?" asked Iona in his earpiece.

"You don't know me but I know you."

Emlyn swallowed nervously. He couldn't see past the darkened visor.

"I'm glad I found you." He leaned forward and pulled out the RT unplugging it. "And now we will join Ms McCallum. Let's go."

He held the pistol inside a pocket as they stood silently waiting for the lift to reach reception. Crazy thoughts about making a dash for it popped up uninvited. In the event Emlyn put the keys down on the reception.

"I hope you got some good pictures." Marilyn shouted after them both.

The van door slid open and they both got in. Iona turned in surprise. "What's going on?" Capello pushed Emlyn into a chair and sat down.

"You two have led me a merry dance and now you have delayed my departure. I hate not running to schedule. I have one last job to do."

He took out the black Heckler & Koch USP pistol from his pocket as Iona's eyes widened.

"Now you're both supposed to be dead so if I killed you what would change? Nothing. It would simply revert to the status quo. On the other hand Jane doesn't know you're alive so why would I need to kill you? I was impressed when you found Iona Emlyn, truly but tell me just for idle curiosity's sake, how did you survive the explosion?"

"Emlyn saved my life. He saw what looked like a puff of smoke coming from a van and threw me onto the ground. Our table fell over protecting us."

Capello laughed at the irony of the story. He had been sent to Scotland to kill Iona and retrieve something that he had possessed all along, following a lunatic trainee who ends up saving the target.

"Why did Jane send you after me? It doesn't make sense."

"If I told you I would have to kill you. However I promise that if after our little impromptu meeting I find I do have to end your life, I will tell you."

"What do you want?" asked Iona

Capello ignored her. "Emlyn apart from you inexplicably finding Iona, I can't say I'm disappointed in you because I never had high expectations in the first place. Even so changing sides like that tut tut. I know that Jane would be quite happy for me to shoot you here and now. And Iona I detect a baby on the way, quick work Emlyn."

"It's not his what do you want?" she repeated.

"You're lucky. I am in the happy position to be able to offer you a deal. I need some information from you Iona and in return you carry on with this very strange half-life existence you now enjoy with Emlyn and if you don't I will regretfully have to kill you both."

"The three of us," said Emlyn defensively.

"Indeed, the three of you. I would very much like to meet Grace Ross-Quinn and I want to know where her HQ is."

"Why, what are you going to do?"

"Why is it that some people are only capable of answering questions with a question? Look at it this way. I will find her that's what I do and I'm good at it. I found you two. Now, holding out will only prolong her miserable existence for a short while and end yours prematurely. Is it worth it? It's a no brainer Ms McCallum I spare you and your baby..."

"...And me."

"Yes Emlyn and you and we all go our separate ways."

"Will you promise not to harm her?"

Capello laughed unexpectedly. "If I gave you my word would you accept it?" Iona was silent. "I didn't think so, you're far too intelligent," he said. "Well? What's it going to be?"

"I don't like you. I know your type you don't frighten me."

"Oh dear. If you knew anything about me you would be very frightened."

"How do we know you won't kill us when you have the information?" asked Emlyn.

"Ah the chicken and the egg, which comes first? Because I am a professional and not a psychopath. I don't kill because I enjoy it. I will tie you up ensure that there are no communication devices in the van and by the time you are released the job will be done. So which is it to be Iona?"

She put her hands to her face and a tear trickled out through her fingers down the back of her hand.

"I need time to think."

"There is no time left," he said looking at his watch.

Emlyn put an arm round her as she wiped away the tears. "There is a warehouse..."

Shouting could be heard outside the van and feet running. Someone slammed against the side shaking it followed by hammering on the door. Capello was too late flicking on the lock as it slid open revealing four full combat soldiers pointing guns. Capello slipped his pistol into a pocket.

"What's this? out." They all got outside as two soldiers went inside and looked at the monitors.

"Sarge it's some kind of monitoring van."

Iona turned but Oriel had already gone. A man went passed carrying an injured unconscious woman.

"Have you any weapons here?"

"No," Iona produced an ID card. "We work for the Scottish Government we were monitoring the crowd for trouble makers."

"Well I would suggest you get the hell out of here, especially in your condition Ma'am and you, get a hair-cut."

The army were still firing. People had thrown themselves on the ground it was hard to tell who had been hit. It was a strange surreal scene with Colin caring nothing for his own safety walked through the mayhem. It was like a battle scene the only difference being no uniforms. He had a flashback and imagined an incoming RPG. Helicopters were flying low down. Eventually he reached the entrance to the car park where an attendant was cowering in his locked cubicle. Colin rapped on the window and he stood up.

"Do you have CCTV?" the man nodded, "can I have a look at the tape over the last thirty minutes."

"Who are you?"

"My girlfriend was shot and I think it could have been from up there," he said pointing.

"The police should be here asking these questions."

Colin pointed over his shoulder. "You can see they've got their hands full."

The attendant replayed the tape, only seven vehicles and a motorbike had left. He looked at each one carefully, an elderly couple, a young girl, a middle-aged man in a sports car. He went through all the images and decided it had to be the motorcyclist. "Can you print off the sharpest frame from the motorbike?" The attendant handed him the print. "Thank you I'm very grateful," he said looking up.

He climbed the stairs until he reached the flat roof and walked over to the edge. This was the perfect spot. The gravel had been disturbed enough to convince Colin he had found the exact place where the marksman had fired his shot. This was a professional hit. Only someone with a great deal of training with the right equipment would be able to hit a target over half a mile away. He looked at the image of the bike. The number plate was clearly legible though that might not get him very far. Still he knew someone who could check it out for him. But the whole thing didn't make sense why would a trained killer go to all these lengths just to shoot Jenny. What was she saying before she was hit? There was such a racket going on when the army started firing he hadn't heard her properly.

"What happened just now?" asked Iona.

"What's wrong with my hair?"

Iona reached over and slapped his arm.

"Stop hitting me I could have an accident. I was filming on the roof and I heard someone say my name. I turned and he was standing there. I have no idea how he found me. He forced me to come to the van. I'm sorry I thought he was going to kill me. Things were bad at the demonstration people were panicking and running about, I heard gunshots."

Iona was retrieving Grace's number on her phone as they drove south towards Bridge of Allan.

"Grace, someone from London tracked us down and he's after you and the department."

"Who?"

I haven't got time to tell you all of that just now but your life is in danger. Remember the video clip from my phone."

"Yes."

"That could be him, same size and build. We didn't get a chance to see his face he was wearing a motorcycle helmet with the visor down. The image should still be on my computer."

"Where are you?"

"We're almost at Bridge of Allan, we'll pick up our stuff and get back right away. We have to find this guy and stop him permanently he's armed and extremely dangerous. I would suggest that if you have any acquaintances that have a spare bed, stay there for now. Can we have a meeting first thing tomorrow morning for debriefing and it would be helpful if we have someone from ops there as well...Em pull in just here."

Emlyn slowed down and stopped outside a fish and chip shop. "...I have to go Grace, I'm starving."

Iona got out of the van and returned swiftly holding a large fish supper with pickled onions and something that was deep fried. She started eating the pickled onions as they drove off.

"What's that?"

"Deep fried coconut shrimp."

"And that?"

"It's a deep fried Mars bar. Have a bite."

They ate in silence as they approached the town. "That's better I was getting the jitters and beginning to lose concentration."

19

"It's 4.0pm, you're watching the 24 hour News Channel updated every 15 minutes and I'm Alison Holt. Fears are growing of a major incident in Stirling where there are reports of people having been fired on by security forces causing many fatalities. The first indication of trouble came when the army began firing live ammunition followed by tear gas. It is not clear what their targets were. There had been no sign of missile throwing or anything else that would seem to have triggered the response however police say that several of their officers were shot. Ambulances had difficulty getting through the crowds that were running away from the troops in panic and reports are coming in of bodies strewn around the park. At its peak the police estimated over a million people were at the demonstration. There are still as many as 500,000 people still occupying the far end of the park next to the bandstand. The police have refused access to our cameras and there is still a ban on flying over the area however many people recorded what happened on their phones and uploaded the images. Gunfire confusion smoke and panic as women and children get caught up in a frightening stampede to get away from the firing. Our correspondent David McFarlane is live at Forth Valley Royal Hospital in Larbert. David the ambulances seem to keep arriving how many people have been taken to A&E?"

"It's impossible to tell because there is chaos here, the injured are lining the corridors waiting to be seen and the operating theatres are going non-stop with teams of surgeons, the scale of this is hard to gauge. Police Scotland have given no details about numbers of casualties so far but they are expected to release a statement very soon. Trying to determine how many people are dead and injured is very difficult but earlier I spoke to Doctor Jāyah who was one of many medical staff drafted in from Edinburgh."

"It's horrific. It is like a war zone, we are so busy treating people we have not had time to even think about numbers but they are high, very high and indiscriminate, many women and children with bullet wounds. It's truly shocking that this could happen in Scotland. This is like a war crime only there is no war. As you can see the corridors are lined with trolleys of the injured waiting for surgery, I must go."

"Well I can tell you that within the last few minutes I have received a statement from Police Scotland saying that quote:

'Following the shooting of four riot policemen, shots were fired in the air by the army to disperse the crowd. So far sixty-three people have been killed with a further one hundred and twelve injured. We should warn the public that these figures may rise. It is too early to attribute a cause of death in all of these cases. We earnestly request that those who are still here should go home to avoid any further trouble.'

It is emerging that this has been to all intents and purposes a massive and deadly blunder by the security forces against unarmed civilians including women and children on a scale that is in the words of Doctor Jāyah truly shocking. The only conclusion at this early stage is that live ammunition was intentionally fired at the crowd. Since the camera crews were kept away from the demonstration it is impossible to challenge or verify exactly what happened but I think there is no doubt in anyone's' mind here that something truly awful happened here today, something that will have reverberations around the world."

"Thank you David McFarlane. Well the shock-waves are already being felt in Westminster with furious exchanges and scuffles breaking out between SNP MP's and government front-benchers in a hastily recalled House of Commons, over to our political correspondent Joyce Paige, Joyce what's been happening?"

"Understandably the Scottish MPs are furious with just about everything the UK government has done but now they are apoplectic with rage at this latest news of a possible massacre of civilians peacefully demonstrating. There are calls of war crimes and resign amongst other sentiments that can't be repeated and it's true to say that the speaker has in effect lost control of procedure at the moment. A number of government back-benchers are extremely concerned at the escalating violence and of the possibility of a revenge attack."

"Ok thanks for that Joyce Paige. Now onto a quick review of the early Evening papers and of course as you would expect they are dominated by today's appalling loss of life at Stirling. 'Massacre of the innocents' with some fairly graphic images that we have had to pixelate. 'Slaughter at Stirling' 'Slaughter as troops rampage in carnival crowd.' 'Dozens mown down by troops' and on the inside there's a story about a statement released by the French President that there will be an immediate blockade of English exports to France. More overseas reaction, and the European Union is holding an emergency meeting to discuss the implications of the violence in Scotland and whether the EU can continue trading with Britain if the violence escalates. The UK ambassador to the US has been summoned to the White House to explain why the situation in the UK appears to be out of control. Poland has expressed concerns for 60,000 Poles living in Scotland with fears for their safety. The strongest condemnation however has come from Canada calling for the PM to be tried for war crimes. At the UN Security Council, China and Russia have condemned the slaughter and proposed that a UN peace keeping force is sent to Scotland. So where will this end? With me is Professor Malcolm McGillivray of Stirling University who is a member of the Government's think tank on predictive analysis and projections, Professor what are the options now facing Scotland and England?"

"Well it's interesting to note that the international community are hardening their stance because of the appalling carnage. I believe that this will be a tipping point. The question really is, tipping point for what? An all-out war between the two countries? A realization by Westminster that their adventure in Scotland is seriously back-firing and possibly a reconciliatory position that in effect allows Scotland to go its own way, I don't know. It is as finally balanced as that. If common sense prevailed there should be a de-escalation of the military presence, a cooling off period to allow politicians to speak to each other and then maybe we might be getting somewhere, but fundamentally at the heart of all of this is a determination by the PM not to allow the break-up of the UK. What it would take to persuade him otherwise who knows but we may have reached a situation whereby in a sense the decision is almost out of his reach. Judging by the sounds coming from allies and others abroad a subjugated Scotland will not be tolerated."

"Stick your neck out Professor what do think will happen?"

"If I was coming to a decision based on logic, graphs, precedence and what's best for both countries that would be easy. But when political decisions are made all bets are off. My advice to the PM would be to allow Scotland full independence with an impartial judicial enquiry into what went wrong then maybe just maybe we could move on."

The Ducati weaved through the slow moving traffic as if it wasn't there and cleared Stirling easily, heading south. Capello had taken a note of the registration number of the van and decided to press on to Edinburgh. There was little point in updating Jane about McCallum and Llewellyn, neither were a threat and as far as he was concerned the job was done and paid for. The traffic ahead had stopped. Now all he had to do was find the van that would most likely be near a warehouse. Then he saw the reason for the long tailback, a police roadblock half a mile ahead checking every vehicle. He stopped not being able to pass between two cars and looked into an Alfa Romeo Giulietta where a young boy was picking his nose and wiping it on the window. He spotted Capello and stuck out his tongue. Capello looked along the line of vehicles, he knew that if they stopped him they would find the rifle. He leaned forward and looked up to see a circling police helicopter.

It was now time to find out how fast this Ducati could go. He moved between the cars onto the hard shoulder and was soon doing a 120mph passing the police checkpoint. It must have seemed like a blur. The road ahead was clear because all the traffic had been held back allowing him to let it rip. Two high speed police cars raced after him, a Lexus IS-F capable of 168 mph and a Jaguar XF top speed 155mph. Oriel looked at the dial and saw he was up to 180mph but felt there was still plenty of grunt left. He judged that they would have radioed ahead and at some point try to intercept if he continued through to Edinburgh. 192mph and the engine was singing, the adrenalin was rushing he hadn't felt like this since he borrowed his uncles 250cc and raced around his home village scaring everybody. 196 mph and he saw what he was looking for, a motorway exit ahead. He looked back and up but there was no sign of chasing vehicles or helicopters. He slowed down and left the motorway at junction seven heading for Kincardine Bridge. It was better to go the long way round rather than straight into Edinburgh.

It was a newly built police station. Constance Black was shown into a large room with two modern laminated tables pushed together with eight comfortable black padded chairs, two on each side. Tiled overhead lights lit the pale green walls one with a single radiator and three more chairs. Above the chairs was a large round chrome plastic clock that had stopped at eleven minutes to twelve. Full length glass sliding doors led out to a balcony overlooking a gravel courtyard with decorative plants below. One door had been left ajar letting in some welcoming fresh air. This was more like a briefing room than an interrogation room. The uniformed officer took up a position opposite her, leaning against the radiator and watched her without expression. Constance walked over to the window, it was getting late in the day with long shadows deepening as the sun slowly continued its downward arc. She knew there was no point asking him questions he was only an escort. There was something strange, something different about this place. She had been in many police stations for one lawful reason or another as part of her job but it wasn't like this. Apart from the distant motorway traffic there was hardly any sound the kind of sound you'd expect in a busy police station. Two men and a woman entered. The woman smiled at Constance and asked her to sit. The men were carrying folders that they put on the table. It was a prop she thought, a piece of authority that they could shelter behind, it must be stressful interviewing people for the first time. The woman was clearly the highest ranking of the four in the room.

"Acting First Minister..."

"...Please call me Connie."

"Connie."

"If this is about the Bell Common bombing, firstly I abhor violence even if there was no one injured and secondly I know absolutely nothing that can help you catch the criminals. If I did I would."

"My name is Chief Superintendent Greenwood this is Detective Sargent Laurel and Detective Pearson..." She hesitated, "I could do with a cup of tea would you like some?"

"That would be lovely."

Greenwood turned to look at the standing uniformed officer who nodded and left. "I'm afraid I'm the bearer of very bad news and I suggest you brace yourself. A number of people were killed at the Stirling demonstration."

"How many?"

Greenwood wouldn't be hurried. "Several riot police were injured and it appears that the army may have over-reacted."

"How many?"

The unmistakeable sound of a helicopter got louder, came into view and landed on the roof. Greenwood stood up and pulled across the sliding door sealing out the noise. She stood at the other side of the table and looked at her open folder. "Seventy-two people killed and one hundred and eighty-three injured some of them badly. The death toll will rise."

"What?"

Greenwood sat down. "There is going to be an investigation."

Constance Black was stunned. "I can scarcely believe it. All these poor people and their families." she cupped her hands to her face.

The door opened and in came the officer carrying a tray with a plain red pottery teapot with matching cups and saucers, a small red milk jug and sugar bowl and placed it on the table.

"Things could very quickly spiral out of control, said Greenwood. "Many, many more could die of their injuries." Her mobile rang. "Oh really?...Thank you. That helicopter you saw landing has brought the head of the British Government's civil service, Sir Jeremy Cottles to speak to you. Is that ok?"

"Yes, of course," she said recovering.

"Come with me?"

The corridors were all but empty. "Where is everybody?"

"Oh this is a brand new station the staff haven't transferred yet."

They continued along corridors up stairs, through swing doors until they reached the Area Commander's office on the top floor. Sir Jeremy Cottles was waiting. The iron rule of the civil service relied on his quick witted Marmite wisdom that divided the staff into two distinct groups those who hated and feared him and those who followed his every word.

"Ms Black I am very pleased to meet you," he said holding out his hand. "I hope your short time here hasn't been too uncomfortable. Please have a seat." The tray had followed them from the briefing room and was set down on the desk. Cottles began pouring. "Milk and sugar?"

"No thanks."

"Thank you Chief Superintendent."

They took the hint and left. Cottles studied Connie.

"These are troubling times Ms Black." There was no 'call me Connie' now. "You've heard about Stirling?" Connie nodded. "Dreadful business, dreadful."

"Why are you here Sir Jeremy?"

"Well," He waved his hands, "you can regard me as a sounding board for the Prime Minister and in order that we can have a full and frank assessment of where we are and how we can resolve the situation that we find ourselves in and proceed, we should feel free to talk."

"You have no one else you can speak to."

"Precisely so and I intend to be uncharacteristically blunt. There are no recordings we have complete privacy. Whatever we agree here in the event that we do will be agreed formally later. I have already given my advice to the Prime Minister about defusing the tensions between our two countries which he is considering. Whether he acts on them or not is entirely a different matter. What happened at Stirling was a total disgrace. Those responsible will be found and punished. I'm not going to speculate about the ins and outs of the lead up to the Stirling massacre however there is a preliminary indication that there is a serious issue within our security services."

"I'm sorry I don't buy that. The security service hierarchy is based on the civil service and there is an inbuilt safeguard from rogue heads of department. Sir Jeremy, there has been a sustained campaign of violence in an attempt to divide Scotland. I believe that No 10 sanctioned the destruction of the Scottish Office Building and also the assassination of our First Minister. The Bell Common tunnel explosion may have been a reaction to that but if it was a revenge attack it was entirely without the knowledge or agreement of my Government."

"The PM is appalled at the level of violence at Stirling and he is deeply concerned that it will lead to a civil war. There are already calls on social media for an army to be raised to protect the people of Scotland. I have to say here and now it has gone too far. He needs a calming influence, someone who will be listened too, not just in Scotland but at Westminster. You will be released of course. You know the civil service walks on a tightrope. We advise when advice is sought but the advice is frequently ignored, however I have advised the PM in the strongest possible way that this cannot go on."

"No country has broken the chains of oppression without sacrifice. I would expect the immediate release of members of my Government that are being held prisoner. The withdrawal of troops. An agreement that Scotland is a sovereign country. That those responsible for the deaths and injury of many people will be found and prosecuted up to and including the Prime Minister and the Home Secretary. I understand that a great many countries shocked by what has happened have offered support including military support. I do not want this. I am willing to enter into negotiations with the Prime Minister but the provocation must stop. Otherwise those who are of a mind unlike mine will feel there is a case for accepting such aid." She shook her head, "it will mean more people dying, this time on both sides. Sir Jeremy, you looked shocked. Did you not realize it takes a great deal of planning and expertise to orchestrate the events over the last month?"

"Do you mind if I write some notes," he said taking out a pad and pen, "you understand a sounding board has little powers."

Connie grimaced, "like the Scottish Government."

20

"Hello Bri." The video link in Cyber-Sam's internet café was good. Brian Peacock moved closer peering at the screen. He was wearing a light blue shirt and pink tie with red braces.

"Colin? You look terrible, is that blood on your shirt?"

"Yes not mine. How's the family?"

"They're fine thanks. Things are a lot better since I stopped travelling and got a desk job. I heard you had some problems."

"Yeah not serious ones, I'm being seen by a shrink."

"How's Pat?"

"We split up some time ago I'm seeing someone else her name's Jenny."

"I never properly thanked you for what you did. We kinda lost touch."

"Yeah I know, what are you doing these days?"

"Same old, only I see my family regularly. I push MI green code to ops, can't say too much over an open link."

"I need a big favour. I'm at the Forth Valley Royal Hospital. Jenny was targeted by a sniper a pro, God knows why. I've got the number plate of his motorbike. Can you track it down for me?"

"Shouldn't you hand it over to the police?"

"It's chaos here."

"I could get the sack."

"I know, I wouldn't ask if there was any other way. It's not political, purely personal."

There was silence as Brian picked up a mug of coffee and took a sip. Colin wiped his mouth.

"Look you're right, I'm out of order it's not fair of me to ask." He looked around to see if anyone was paying attention then back to the screen. He was just about to break the link when Brian spoke.

"What's the number?"

Colin told him. "I'm sticking around here to be near Jenny. I don't have a mobile but I've got hers." And he gave Bri the number. "Thanks mate and now I owe you." Colin made his way back to the Emergency Department and couldn't find Jenny. "Excuse me Doctor?..."

"...Dr Jāyah."

"Yes, I'm looking for Jenny Leask? I'm her partner."

"You've just missed her she's gone to the Acute Assessment Unit. She may have gone straight into surgery."

"Is there anyone I can talk to?"

Dottie checked her mobile touched the screen and smiled at him. "Hello its Dr Jāyah do you have Jenny Leask, I think she's in surgery...she was in surgery that was quick...good...I have her partner here...Ok. She's recovering from surgery it was quick and straight forward. I didn't see her when she came in but I was told that if her arrival had been delayed she would not have survived."

"Thanks," he said shaking her hand. "Thanks very much."

"Ok what happened?"

They were in a briefing room with small windows looking out to a brick wall. Grace was standing with her palms on the table Iona, Emlyn and Jonathan Ingles from ops were seated. He was taking notes.

"We checked out all the gear in the van," Emlyn began. "The links etc. and it was all working Ok. I asked for permission from a receptionist to go on the roof of a building that had a good view below. I found the target group and started streaming images to Iona. I heard someone call my name behind me and when I turned round it was a motorcyclist still wearing his helmet and visor. I'm afraid I can't remember what he said, it just seemed surreal."

"I heard him over the link Grace and wrote it down," said Iona. "He said, 'Hello Emlyn you don't know me but I know you, I'm glad I found you.' Then I lost the link. Next thing I know the door is flung open and they both came in. He threatened us with a pistol and wanted to know about you and where this place was. He said he would kill us if I didn't tell him. Fortunately some soldiers opened the van door and told us to get out. They were very nervous. This guy disappeared when we were talking to them. You're a target now and I have no doubt he was sent by Jane Caddish. He knew about us being in the Diner explosion, wanted to know how we survived it. I think he was sent to track Emlyn to kill me."

Grace sat down. "He'll know the number of the van I'm sure, just as well it's tucked away in the lock-up. Ok this is all beginning to make sense. Four policemen were shot. Expertly targeted so that there would be no fatalities. The riot police take fright and start retreating quickly towards the army. They panic and start firing not knowing where the shots were coming from. Some fired in the air some fired at imaginary terrorists killing dozens. The rest of the fatalities were as a result of crowd crush as they panicked to get out of the park. Now I think we can safely assume that motorbike Charley was employed to assassinate you and it looks like he was sent to Stirling to provoke a violent reaction at the demonstration, successfully as it happened. If nothing else we can now assume that London was behind the massacre in the park. It must have been entirely coincidental and unfortunate that he saw you Emlyn. You say you were on a roof then he must have also been on a roof. What was nearby?"

Emlyn scratched his head. "I don't know. "Hold on there was a multi-storey car park."

"Jonathan can you check that out?" He nodded.

"One more thing..." Iona paused. "I asked him why he had been sent after me and he said, *'If I told you I would have to kill you. However I promise that if after our little impromptu meeting I find I do have to end your life, I will tell you.'* He knew why Jane sent him after me. Now apart from having access to some servers for a short time that incidentally I don't anymore, I know I did nothing that would warrant a hired killer coming after me, so where does that leave us."

"It could have been him," said Emlyn surprising them all. "He could have stolen something, I don't know, the Crown Jewels?"

"The Crown Jewels," repeated Iona then she started laughing. "The Crown Jewels Emlyn, you really are a genius and you still don't even know it. He's retiring. *'You two have led me a merry dance and now you have delayed my departure. I hate not running to schedule. And now I have one last job to do.'* He's taken something from the firm."

"Iona do you still have Jane Caddish's email address?" asked Grace.

"Yes."

"Ok send her an email." Grace typed it printed it out and handed it over to Iona. "I think that's everything we need to say to Jane for the moment.

'Hello Jane, yes I did survive the American Diner explosion. I have spoken to your hit-man.

1. *We know that he sparked off the Stirling massacre by shooting at the security forces from a multi-storey car park.*
2. *We know that he has a contract on one of our Intel heads.*
3. *We know you think I have stolen the 'Crown Jewels'.*

So regarding:
1. This information may find its way into the public domain if
2. You do not recall him and terminate the contract and
3. We believe he has the 'Crown Jewels.'

Think about this Jane would I be stupid enough to let you know I survived when I could simply have disappeared. You have a rogue agent Jane, do something about it.

Iona.'

"I'm going home Em," said Iona. "To Mum's house."

"What about me?" He was like a helpless confused puppy. "I can't stay with Dottie on my own and what's Jane going to do about me now she knows you're alive?"

"Look, I think you should go home to Cardiff."

"Dolgellau."

"What?"

"Renton came from Cardiff."

"Em, you're like a bad cold I can't get rid of, like a tummy bug that won't go away." Iona saw the expression on his face and immediately felt bad about what she had just said. "ARRGH," she shouted at him. "Oh alright."

Jane Caddish read Iona's email without expression. Nothing really surprised her anymore in the business she was in. She glanced at the papers on her desk bearing the full horror of the killings. She never dreamed that the security forces would be stupid enough to start firing directly into the crowd. There was no way the contract could be rescinded that was one of the unwritten rules. Once a contract had been issued Capello would be unreachable until he decided to contact her. The video link pinged and an image of Sir Brian Mowbray appeared.

"Jane could you come to my office please."

There was no hello Jane how are you pleasantry. It was cold and to the point.

"Yes Sir."

It was a long walk to the Director's office and Jane was slightly out of breath by the time she arrived. She looked at his secretary who nodded for her to enter.

"Sit down Jane," he said without looking up. "No 10 seems to be backtracking. I believe international pressure over the Stirling business has been a game changer. You will have to cut loose your black ops man. No connections, no strings, no ties with GCHQ."

"I'm afraid it might be too late for that sir. One of my analysts that we thought had died in an explosion survived. I have just received an email from her and I believe the contents to be accurate. She knows precisely what has happened and furthermore it appears that he is the one who stole the sensitive information about GCHQ. To protect the department we have to send another agent from Increment to find and stop him from passing on the information."

"See to it Jane. If we're not careful we could find ourselves holding the parcel when the music stops."

"I would like £20m transferred to my Bitcoin wallet," Capello was cleaning his rifle. He glanced at the blank screen waiting for a reply from the encrypted audio internet link. "If you think that's too much I'll shop around." Silence. "Here's the deal. I send you an encrypted folder with everything you need to intercept and listen in to Coms at GCHQ with many extras. Believe me it's the bargain of the century. And after you transfer the Bitcoins, I send you the key."

"How can we trust you?" The voice was East European possibly Albanian.

"Because I know from experience that there is no hiding place if enough commitment is invested. At any rate I don't want to spend the rest of my life looking over my shoulder. Again, I'm not forcing you into the deal I can go elsewhere, this is hot stuff." He leaned back in his chair admiring the rifle, it was immaculate. "Take your time," he said getting up and walking to the window.

He liked Edinburgh. In this transient world there was something reassuringly permanent about the town and its enduring skyline. It had so many

Grecian pillared buildings someone had called it the Athens of the North. He regretted that he couldn't 'disappear' here, that would have been ideal. He looked through the scope, the cross hairs following a cyclist pedalling hard over the cobbles.

"I don't have clearance, I will have to call you back."

Capello sighed. "Ok don't wait too long," he said closing the laptop.

His search for the van revealed that it was a 2013 Mercedes-Benz Sprinter first registered in Perth, the last MOT was six months previously at a garage in Leith. There were warehouses in Leith. He wondered if he had made a mistake approaching Llewellyn. At the time it seemed like a good idea but it may have left him exposed having to leg it when he was interrupted. He closed his eyes and cleared his mind, kneeled on the floor and fell forward catching his weight with down facing palms and began the second of four sessions of press-ups. He hardly broke sweat as it ended. He stood up and opened the fridge took out a bottle of spring water closing the door and unscrewed the top. Body perfect, if he had a motto that would be it. He liked this bit of an assignment, cut off from control, his own master it was a kind of freedom to use his own initiative, the hunter and the hunted. The game couldn't be more exhilarating. Grace would know now she was the quarry that it made it even more interesting. What Capello didn't know was that he was also the quarry with three pursuers.

21

Jenny's flat was sparsely furnished. In polite circles it would have been described as minimalist. On one wall housed in a thin gilt frame slightly askew with a faded print of three kittens in a basket of wool after Henriette Ronner-Knip. The mid nineteen sixties three piece suite covered in a plain charcoal moquette was somewhat threadbare but still comfortable to sit in. The vertical blinds were open revealing Perth wearing its pervasive cloak of inscrutability astride the majestic River Tay. Colin was fond of Perth it was like a big village, a Cinderella desperate to go to the ball. There was very little news ever came out of Perth, nothing it seems that was at all newsworthy ever happened here. In cruel journalistic parlance it was a news Bermuda triangle where anything worth reporting was sucked into an unrecoverable abyss to be lost forever.

Perth the centre of Scotland should have its own international airport but it seemed that its proximity to Dundee precluded it from any such aspirations. Yet it was one of the finest cities in Scotland to live in. It was quiet during the day until the neighbour came home, usually with a skin full and began slapping his timid wife around. Colin promised himself he would have to sort that out sooner or later. The endless reruns of the killing spree on the rolling twenty-four hour news channels was depressing. He called the hospital and was told there was no news except she was slowly getting stronger. He called his parents and told them but kept back the detail in case they were upset. Anger welled up inside him. He searched for his medicine and found one last capsule in his pocket. He would have to get a repeat prescription soon. He closed his eyes and let his head fall back on the cushion. The sound of a cricket began. He opened his eyes. It got louder, it was Jenny's phone.

"Hello?"

"Colin?"

"Yes."

"Brian Peacock. You sound a bit strange everything ok?"

"Yeah, of course."

"OK well you're in luck. We checked out the number and the bike was a hire so we did a CCTV check at the hire company including face recognition and came up with a name..."

Hello?"

"Yes I'm still here."

"This guy has been flagged up by Military Intelligence a few times. His name is Oriel Capello. He's a black hat Colin, best to keep your distance. Given the cover he gets from the establishment I would say he is a member of the Increment. We have been told to avoid them. They are the untouchables."

"I need a lead."

"You're not listening to me."

"Was I ever any good at listening?"

"Once."

"I need to track this guy down."

"Ok do you want to know how many hits he's chalked up?"

"No."

"Ok it's your funeral. I'll text you with what I have."

Colin closed his eyes. The anger was within but it was different this time it was under control. A text alert pinged. He studied the image of his girlfriends attempted killer. Shaved head, no facial hair, brown eyes, a large nose and thin lips with a don't mess with me stare at the camera. He was thirty-nine years old an ex-member of the SAS, licensed to carry a firearm by the Home Office, no address. It still didn't make any sense why he would want to shoot Jenny. Surely he was there for something else. Colin didn't care, it was irrelevant. There would be no questions when he caught him only one solution. He picked up the keys to Jenny's old green Jetta and looked down at it from the window. It had some thick cloth gaffer tape across the bonnet to keep it down and numerous dents and scratches where the rust was beginning to show through. It was never locked. Jenny had joked she didn't care if someone stole it. Still it was better than nothing. The car was parked on a slope because of the faulty starter motor and it needed bump starting. Other than that it mysteriously never broke down. A sharp wind met him as he left the building and walked over to the car. The hinge of the door squeaked on opening and again when he closed it. He put the key in the ignition. There was a tired smell inside, the auto equivalent of the interior of a care home. First stop, the hospital.

"Ladies and gentlemen welcome to Edinburgh. Please ensure that you take all your hand luggage and stay seated with your seat belt fastened until the plane comes to a complete standstill."

Lewis Sebastian Digby, aka the 'Digger' on account of how many people he had put in the ground, looked out of the window at the airport tower resembling a wine decanter. He didn't have to consider whether or not to take on this job it was a job like any other. There was no such thing as a code in Increment. If it wasn't him it would be some someone else. Of course it would be harder since Capello was also a trained assassin and knew all about covering his back. One advantage was that Capello didn't know him indeed that was why he was chosen. Digby was a person with albinism. It wasn't a desirable trait to have if you wanted to disappear in a crowd. As a consequence he dyed his hair and eyebrows but drew the line on colouring his eyelashes. In addition he had the palest blue eyes with the combined result of making him look slightly unusual.

He was known for his patience often tracking someone for weeks until the right moment but now he was working against the clock, his instructions couldn't be clearer. Find Capello recover what was stolen and kill him, simple. He had been told to keep in contact with Colleen Bentsen for updates. It only took a couple of minutes for the shuttle to arrive at the Hilton Edinburgh Airport Hotel where a large package was waiting for him. He signed in under a pseudonym, asked for an upper room, accepted the key-card, told the receptionist he could find the room and made his way to the lift with the heavy package balanced over his shoulder. The room was spacious with a king sized bed, a two seater sofa next to the corner window and a coffee table. He laid the parcel gently down on the table dropped his rucksack on the suitcase stand and looked out the window to the car park. He left the room and checked the exits and fire escapes at either end of the corridor. He returned to his room turned the security latch across and looked at his watch.

He sat on the red sofa and studied the parcel. All he needed was in there and when he was finished it would be disposed of. There was no need to contact London they would know where he was. He took his phone out and connected to a Virtual Private Network through 4g. Any public Wi-Fi was a security risk. There were no messages. He unwrapped the covering of the parcel to reveal a case. He opened it and whistled quietly. There was the beast waiting to be assembled, an Armalite AR-50 with a range of more than a mile and a half weighing in at thirty-four pounds. He checked to see if it was all there. It had a single bolt action with nothing to go wrong. It came with a modified noise and flash suppressor. The weight didn't bother Digby because it was worth it. His fingers traced the cold matt green metal of the precision instrument and marvelled at the beautiful engineering. This was the first time he would use one of these feeling that distance means safety, especially with a quarry like Capello. The room phone rang.

"Sir your hire car has been delivered we have the keys at reception."

Jacqueline Brill took off her ear defenders and put them on a hook while she checked her score.

"Grace you've got to be kidding I thought the SSRR would only react on a matter of extreme emergency that threatened national security."

"Ok my life is not a matter of national security but the guy doesn't have to be killed just...well, neutralised...nullified...cancelled out."

The confrontation was in a fitted out cellar, sound proofed for target practice. Jacqui took off her safety glasses and put them on the same hook.

"Neutralise a trained assassin exactly how do you propose I do that without killing him?"

Jacqui towering over Grace took a hankie out and blew her nose. She was bristling inside and trying to hide her annoyance at being asked to kill someone. The idea that she or anyone in the newly set up Scottish Special Reconnaissance Regiment would deliberately execute someone in cold blood was outrageous.

"You're trained in firearms."

"Of course I am. I shoot dummies at a distance with ear defenders and protective eyewear, I don't shoot these kind of dummies. Grace I don't think you understand this goes against everything I stand for. I'm a Christian did you know that?"

"I've read your file. I also know that you're top of the grade in firearm practise. Look this man has been sent out to assassinate me and probably close this department down. Now stopping him might conflict with your religious beliefs but I don't see it that way. If you don't do your job I will die is that clear enough?"

Jacqui swept a lock of blond hair behind one ear and looked at Grace.

"This is a new world Jacqui," said Grace forcefully. "The stakes are higher, the rewards greater. I don't care if anything happens to me. What is more important is the self determination of a sovereign Scotland. I would gladly die if it meant that future generations were free to choose their own destiny. If anyone can get close to this guy it's you and if you choose not to..."

"...Ok, ok but let me deal with him in my own way."

"Only on one condition. You do not put your life at risk."

"Grace that's a bit like telling me to stop a bus by jumping in front of it but don't get hurt. If this guy is a pro he's not going to be thinking about anything other than finding you and finishing off the job. What about the legal thing, how is that going to play out because there's a difference between taking out a hit-man and plain murder."

"The situation is this. The SSRR was created for just these kinds of operations admittedly for action outside the country, but it's a necessity for the security of an independent Scotland. As you know there is a certain ambiguity about that going on and actions taken by members of the SSRR would in the present scenario be illegal."

"In other words there is no legal reason that I would not be convicted of murder unless it was self-defence."

"There you have it Jacqui, you've got the answer clever you, I knew you would. Is your licence to carry a concealed weapon up to date?"

She checked the slimline Glock 36, ejected the single-stack magazine and loaded a fresh one with its six .45 calibre rounds. The weapon specially designed for concealment slipped into her shoulder holster and she put on an unfastened waistcoat to hide it. Grace was annoyed at being made to wait.

"Yes of course. How do I find this guy?"

"You won't need to he'll find me."

"Great you're going to be the bait! Grace I don't like it what if it goes wrong?"

"I'll waken up dead and most likely so will you. Now there is a further complication." Grace looked at Jacqui who had put her hands on her hips.

"London might also be looking for chummy as well. It appears he has taken something that didn't belong to him."

"What?"

"I don't know but if you get to him first, get it."

"Great, is there anything else I should know about?"

Grace paused. "Well yes, the manager of the motorbike hire company in London said that we were the third to ask about the CCTV images of the driver. So it appears that there is someone else looking for him. I'm afraid that our targets' face didn't flag up an ID but you can have a copy of it along with what little we have upstairs."

"So how do we entice him in?"

"Well firstly there is a small empty warehouse not far from here. We'll get the van out of the cellar car park and leave it outside this warehouse when we're ready. If he was doing his job right he would have taken a note of the registration number and he would know that the MOT was last done in Leith. So he'll be looking for it here."

"I'm not trying to back out but it sounds very much like a job for the heavy boys."

"Can't trust them, can't trust anybody outside. Learn that lesson and learn it well."

22

"She is very very lucky. The bullet narrowly missed a main artery and lodged next to it in the muscle. It couldn't have been any closer," the surgeon said. "Getting her here fast probably saved her life."

"Can I see it."

"What?"

"The bullet."

"it's being kept for evidence. We notified the police, every gunshot injury is notifiable, but the police have been overwhelmed they haven't seen yet."

Colin looked at her name badge. "Please Nurse Greig."

She looked tired. She slid open a cabinet door and took out a little plastic beaker with the bullet inside and handed it to Colin.

"I used to be in the army," he said looking at the bullet. "Whenever the police do show up you can tell them it's a .338 Lapua Magnum cartridge. A snipers' bullet probably from a Remington MSR. Thanks," he said handing it back. "Can I see her."

"Of course but she will get tired easily."

Nurse Greig led the way into a four bed ward. They were all occupied. Jenny was in the corner next to a large window. She was propped partially upright with a drip attached to the back of her hand and gave him a weak smile as he approached. He kissed her and pulled over the light brown simulated leather armchair and sat down.

"I hear it was touch and go," he said

"I'm so pleased to see you."

"What do you remember about Saturday?"

"People panicking, screaming and running. I saw him."

"What?"

Jenny nodded. "He was on the roof of the multi-storey car park. I saw a flash then another and another. I shouted to you but you couldn't hear me and the last thing I remember is pointing."

".That's why he shot you. I saw the bullet he was a sniper, an army marksman trained to fire a very specialized weapon. He must have been the one who shot the police and he saw you pointing. Didn't your mother ever tell you that it was rude to point?"

"What have you been doing?"

"I..." Colin stopped should he tell her that a friend in Military Intel had helped him out and he intended to find the sniper, and then what? "We should get married." He took her free hand and kissed it.

Jenny's eyes widened, "is that a proposal?"

"Don't you want to get married?"

There was silence in the ward as the other patients and visitors listened for an answer. Jenny pulled her hand away. "Colin Alexander Reid, you're an idiot." Someone giggled.

"For goodness sake man, do it properly," said an elderly man with no teeth pointing a stick at Jenny.

Colin smiled and went on one knee holding her hand again. "Will you marry me?" A loud cheer went round the ward.

"Of course I will you big lummock."

Iona was depressed. Not just fed up but seriously fed up. If Bjørge had been around he would have got it. She wasn't sleeping well, she was anxious and the tears could come at any time. The comfort of being at home helped but she hated the feeling and it wasn't at all her. She had snapped at Emlyn for no reason and hated herself for doing it. She couldn't face the food Emlyn had cooked though it was perfectly alright and she was tired. She wanted to stay in bed and didn't even want to leave the house.

"I've been reading about antenatal depression," said Emlyn cheerfully chewing on a piece of shortbread, "it's quite common."

She was sitting at the kitchen table and without warning burst into tears. Emlyn moved over and put his arm round her.

"I don't like seeing you like this, you're a tough guy," he said. "Look I know you don't think very much of me and let's face it what is there to like but I am very fond of you. No that's not right, I love you. We've been through a helluva lot and what I'm trying to say and making a fist of it as usual is that if there is anything that I can do, anything at all to help I would be only too happy to...well help," he ended lamely.

"I called you some bad things, I'm sorry."

"I've been called worse."

"Em do you have...have you had a girlfriend?"

"Well not exactly."

"God you're a virgin."

"Iona that's none of your business," he said withdrawing his arm.

There was an uneasy silence that neither wanted but it was a kind of truce, a space to regroup, reassess their complicated relationship.

"I'm sorry Em, antenatal depression."

"No, you don't get off that lightly," he said with the hint of a twinkle in the eye.

Iona leaned over and kissed him on the lips. "Don't read anything into that," she said with a smile. "OW. That was a real kick."

She was holding her swollen stomach. Emlyn stood up and held her round the waist kissing her full on the mouth. Only a muffled protest could be heard from her that stopped. She relaxed and put her arms round his neck returning his kiss. It was so intense they weren't aware of a key finding a lock until the front door opened letting in the sound of the main street traffic. They sprang apart in surprise. Iona went into the hall as Bjørge came in. They both stood looking at each other in disbelief.

"What are you doing here?" they said in unison. Iona went forward and kissed and hugged him.

"I didn't expect to see you here. I came to Edinburgh to find you," he said.

"You should have let me know."

"You would have just told me to stay in Norway and I couldn't because I wanted to..."

Emlyn appeared at the end of the hall, "...who's this?"

"Oh this is Emlyn Bjørge, Bjørge, Emlyn."

"Is he staying here?"

"I've heard a lot about you," said Emlyn.

"Well you have me at a disadvantage I've heard nothing about you."

"He's here for the time being."

"I don't understand."

"Come in to the kitchen and I'll make you a coffee."

Iona put the kettle on as Bjørge sat down. Emlyn stood by the sink studying him.

"Well don't you think there should be some kind of explanation?"

"Emlyn is business."

"I slept with Iona," he said.

"EMLYN," she shouted.

"Twice."

Iona's eyes went to the ceiling. "Nothing happened," she said.

"Business?" said Bjørge. The electric kettle boiled and clicked off.

"I love you Iona and I want to marry you," said Emlyn. "I saved her life," he said to Bjørge.

"Will you just shut up?"

"Before you came in..." he started.

"...Emlyn is a virgin."

"Wait, wait, it's too much information. Maybe I should go out wait five minutes and come back in again because I feel like I've fallen down a rabbit hole with Alice in Wonderland. Iona how do you know he's a virgin? And why is that important?"

Iona sat next to Bjørge who was visibly shaken. She looked at him and chewed the inside of her lip something she didn't do very often.

"I am, so glad you're here. I really, really missed you. A lot has happened since you left. Did you read about the American Diner bomb?" He nodded, "I was there having breakfast when Emlyn came in. He was sent by SIS to find me. Somehow he spotted a van outside that was about to explode and pushed me onto the floor. Our table overturned shielding us from the blast. London thought we had both died in the explosion. We stayed with Dottie do you remember me talking about her?" he nodded again. "Nothing has happened between Emlyn and me. I felt the baby move one night and he came through to ask if I was alright and he felt the baby kicking and it was a comfort thing like a comfort blanket having someone next to me. I know it sounds bad and I know I shouldn't have, but absolutely nothing happened."

"Uhuh and the second time?"

"We were at Stirling. The B&B I booked for Emlyn was full and because of the demonstration there was nowhere else to go. It was a double bed and we used a bolster between us."

"A what?"

"A bolster, it's like a long pillow we used three. And nothing happened. Now," she said turning to Emlyn, "is that all correct?"

"Unfortunately, yes."

"I believe you. I don't know how, maybe that's just the way I am. I came to find you because I wanted to ask you to marry me."

"You can't marry him Iona, I asked you first," said Emlyn.

"It's not first come first served," said Bjørge.

"Em could you excuse us for a minute?" asked Iona.

"No I'm serious. I do love you and I want to marry you and I don't care if you tie me to a wind turbine until my brain turns to mince."

"What on earth are you talking about? Right that settles it. In Norway we have a way of deciding matters of the heart. I challenge you to a duel."

Iona started laughing but there was no smile on Bjørge's face.

"Don't be ridiculous?" she said.

"Normally it's duelling pistols. I don't have any but I'm also very good with swords. Do you accept?"

"You're not serious," said Emlyn.

"Deadly," he said perhaps not selecting Emlyn's preferred word of choice.

Emlyn looked at Iona and back at Bjørge. "Swords it is."

"Ok this has gone far enough if you two keep on with this silly duel thing I'll not marry either of you. No that's wrong wait a minute. Emlyn I am not going to marry you even if you were to kill Bjørge in this fantasy duel that in any case will never happen and Bjørge yes I will marry you. That's an end to it. And Em I'm afraid you're going to have to go."

Emlyn's face crumpled. "Where to?"

"Cardiff."

"It's Dolgellau! What will I do?"

Bjørge shook his head. "For goodness sake Emlyn, man-up and get your own, nice Welsh girl."

23

He gave the taxi driver a hundred pounds and told him to keep driving until the money ran out. They toured the streets, the narrow back lanes, avenues, crescents, places, squares, in Leith. They passed every pub, library, school, block of flats sometimes twice. The driver was satisfied that his fare was house hunting and wanted to know all about Leith. At first it was interesting. The cabbie took to his newfound job as tour guide with gusto. His relentless descriptions of the buildings as they passed became a drone. He took a great pride in revealing his intimate and voluminous knowledge of Leith even to the most detailed obscure minutiae. Capello glanced at the meter. There was probably another hour and a half to go. Along Leith walk, Easter Road passing Hib's football ground for the second time they continued until he asked the driver to stop. "What's along there?" He pointing towards a cobbled lane.

"It's a cul-de-sac, there's only a line of warehouses, it's a dead end."

"I like dead ends." They travelled on the bumpy cobbled road and turned a corner.

"Stop," there was a black Mercedes van parked outside a warehouse. He checked the number and it matched. Oriel scanned the buildings on both sides of the narrow street.

"Do you know what these warehouses are being used for?"

"All different businesses. Sometimes they share the same warehouse. Businesses like media production, electronics, software designers, new tech I call it. Just about everything."

"Ok can you reverse back?"

The driver turned round puzzled. "It would be easier if I turned at the end."

"I think I've found what I'm looking for." He reached into his pocket and took out a fifty pound note. "Here's a bonus. Now I would prefer you to reverse back."

The driver took the note and shrugged. "For this kind of money I'll reverse you all the way home."

He dropped him three blocks away from the flat as requested. Capello had time to form a plan while walking. Of course it was too easy. He was meant to find the van and then what? A trap? They wouldn't just leave a link to Grace lying outside their HQ. He arrived and entered searching for equipment in has bag and found the night-scope. He had noted that there weren't many lamp posts in the lane. If they were carrying out a twenty-four hour stakeout there would be shifts and that would be his chance. He found a fake driving licence that would bear scrutiny and a currently valid credit card and phoned a hire car company booking a diminutive three door Kia Picanto with details from the credit card. An email alert pinged on his mobile.

'We agree to your terms, £20m in Bitcoins will be transferred to your Bitcoin wallet. Send the encrypted folder now and your Bitcoin address and when the transactions are complete send the encryption key to open the folder. Remember if we do not receive the encryption key we will find you. There will be no hiding place.'

Capello took out his laptop and plugged in the drive. In seconds he had sent the folder. He looked at his watch and waited. Maybe they were going to use brute strength to break the encryption. That was always a possible scenario he had to accept. He looked at his watch again, he couldn't wait any longer he had to go. He unplugged the drive and put it in his pocket.

"What are you doing here? Shouldn't you be on maternity leave?"

Grace was wearing another new dress. It was a loose fitting floral number that wouldn't have been out of place on holiday in Hawaii. She had a matching scarf around her neck.

"I had to get out of the house Bjørge is back. That didn't sound right. We're going to get married."

"Wasn't that a little awkward with Emlyn staying with you?"

"Yes for a while. Could have been a lot worse. I'm lucky with Bjørge he's not at all the jealous type, I wish he was sometimes."

"Ok back to business, I have someone from special ops who's staking out your coms van parked outside a deserted warehouse when this guy turns up she'll be ready for him."

"She?"

"Yeah, Iona there's no gender discrimination here and she is a damn fine shot. I would trust her with my life and I probably will have to."

"Grace please, I don't mean this in any disparaging way but how did you find yourself head of this department?"

"By default. There was no one else. My speciality is game development you know the baddies against the goodies. Space aliens, cowboys and Native Americans, war fare, good against evil so what's different? We're fighting a war here and whatever my political affiliations which is between me and the ballot box, this is the job that I do for my employers. Strange you don't seem to know much about civil servants, that's how it works. Why are you here you should be safely at home?"

"I worry about you."

Grace laughed, "go home Iona, please you shouldn't be here."

"I want to help."

There was the slightly theatrical sound of throat being cleared. "I'd like to help too," said Emlyn taking off his coat.

"Alright we need round the clock surveillance of the Coms van, ok?"

"Of course."

"What do they pay you Iona?"

"I don't know yet I haven't checked."

"It's not enough," said Grace.

"Why don't you go home to Bjørge, I'll take your shift."

"You were already factored in Emlyn. Oh by the way have a word with James he might be able to find you a place to stay." Emlyn had avoided looking at Iona and nodded then walked off to James desk.

"I don't mind, I'd rather keep busy."

Colleen Bentsen was polishing her nails. It was a calming ritual something that she felt was good for her psychological well-being rather than just looking good. Vanity perhaps, femininity yes. She had noticed that others at GCHQ had sneered in the politest way possible but she didn't care. Coming from a working class background in Belfast she was immune to the privileged view. They also thought that someone who cared so much about appearance was in some way, wanting. Her department was full of the privately educated elite and that was Ok aside from the erroneous class judgements. It was a chip not a very big one but nevertheless it was still there on the shoulder. She was dying for a fag and it was distracting her. She took a deep breath and stared at her monitor. Capello had used a listed credit card to hire a car. She called Jane.

"Ma'am Capello's card has been used to hire a car."

It was a curt reply, "pass it on to Digby."

There was a tap at the window. Colin was lying down on the back seat of Jenny's old VW Jetta and woke up stiff and cold to see a policeman looking in. He wound down the window a little letting in the cold night air. The open twenty-four hour Asda car park was almost empty apart from a few staff cars.

"Sorry pal, you can't doss here, you'll have to move on."

Colin took the keys out of the ignition got out of the car and stood next to it. "I've nowhere to go. Can you just turn a blind eye I'll be gone in the morning?"

"We'll have to nick you if you stay here."

"You can't nick a customer of Asda's it might get in the papers."

"We're not stopping you going in to Asda."

"Ok," Colin put his hands in his pocket and started to walk away.

"Hey you haven't locked the door."

"It doesn't lock."

The supermarket was empty of customers except for a small elderly woman with all the time in the world. "Are you alright love?" he asked.

"I'm waiting for my niece and then we're going home for lunch. I hope it's not fish again, I don't like the bones."

Colin walked between the aisles stacked with things he couldn't afford. The annoyingly loud music berating the two 'customers' was Badfinger's lyrics. '...If you want it here it is come and get it but you better hurry cause it may not last'. The irony of the lyrics made him smile until physical hunger began gnawing at him again. He had long recognized emotional hunger. That he could ignore. He started shaking and his concentration wavered with the lowering blood sugar. He resisted the temptation to grab a packet of sausage rolls and eat them there and then and if he got arrested so what. But he couldn't get arrested because he had a job to do. He went to the toilet well aware security would be tracking him round the store from camera to camera. He washed his face and hands and tried to pat down his sticking up hair. His mirror image did nothing to dissuade an opinion that he may have been sleeping under a hedge. He walked back towards the exit via a line of Ultra HD television sets showing preposterously beautiful images of the Mojave Desert in spring. He stopped at the news-stand but the papers hadn't arrived yet. There was an assistant behind the counter of the kiosk.

"Excuse me dear but there's an old lady who seems to be a bit confused in the store," he said.

"I know that's Margaret we always keep an eye on her to make sure she's Ok. We phoned her sister to pick her up poor thing."

He smiled and made his way outside. The smile froze as he saw that the police car was still there next to his Jetta.

"Come on guys have you not got criminals to catch?"

"Move on we'll not tell you again."

"Ok you win. You'll have to give me a push though the starter motor's not working either."

The driver of the police car wound up the window and drove off across the car park leaving him alone.

24

The sign outside the pub said Bridger's but everyone knew it as Ma Riley's. She had long gone but the name stuck. Now it was her son Doug who had taken over. The bar just off Edinburgh's Rose Street was quiet. Colin had been in once before, meeting up with some Edinburgh pals. Doug poured a half of lager while Colin looked at the shelves of whiskies. Most of them he'd never heard of, it had been a long time since he had tasted any kind of whisky. He fished in his pocket and scraped out some change just enough to pay. He took his drink over to a table where five men waited and sat down.

"Thanks for coming guys, I'm sorry I can't get you a drink, skint."

"You look terrible Colin have you been sleeping rough?"

They were all ex-army apart from Will who had just spoken. He was a serving sergeant on leave. They were all similar ages and been through the same experiences but this wasn't a reunion at least not a proper one.

"Asda car park, I've been sleeping in the car. It's an all-nighter I go in and have a wander around when I'm cold and needing the toilet. I got sanctioned," he said taking a sip. "Anyway you didn't come to hear a sob story and thanks by the way for coming. I need some help."

"You certainly do," said Will, reaching for the wallet in his back pocket.

"No not that kind of help. Jenny's in hospital she was shot by an army marksman," he took another sip of his beer, "we were in Stirling when all those people died. The round they dug out of her was a .338 Lapua Magnum cartridge from a snipers rifle and I want to find him." He took out a picture. "This is the guy. His name is Oriel Capello the family originate from Tarragona in Catalonia. He's a master of Black Ops from the Increment."

"What are they when they're at home?" asked Jim.

"They are seriously bad news."

"Well the best way to find anybody is to predict what they're going to do next. Why was he there?"

"He was the one that sparked off the massacre at Stirling. He was shooting at the riot squad and the army retaliated. Jenny spotted him and ended up in intensive care, she's alright now, thank God."

"So he's working for Secret Intelligence and their plan is to disrupt the independence movement. Who's next on the list that's what we need to find out. Jim you worked in Comms for a while what's Scotland's Intel capability like?" asked Will.

"Everything goes through Cheltenham so if there is any Intel capability here, it's cobbled together. I've got some mates still there, I could find out."

"My cousin's aunt is a clairvoyant," Gordon usually never said very much but when he did nobody paid much attention to it. He raised and shook his arm making his loose wristwatch band slide down.

"Comms have a lot of connections, it might be worthwhile," said Jim ignoring him.

"She's from the Highlands, Ardgay or Bonar I can never remember which. In the Highlands they're called seers," he continued, used to being ignored.

"Gordon shut up," said Will annoyed.

"Really she might be able to help."

"I don't think you're taking this very seriously Gordon," said Colin rubbing the stubble on his jaw.

"I'm deadly serious, she's good. She happens to be staying with Mina in Marchmont just now if you want to meet her I can take you." Colin looked at Will and shook his head.

Will shrugged his shoulders. "It can't do any harm. By the way Colin for goodness sake while you're in Edinburgh stay with us."

The four floor Victorian terraced tenement with bay windows boasted a broken arch pediment over the blue front door. A bike was chained to what was left of a gatepost. Gordon looked at the list of names on the entry pad pressed and waited. Colin pulled up the collar of his jacket against a biting wind that had just sprung up. A dog barked in the distance and music could be heard from one of the flats above.

"Maybe you should have let her know we were coming," said Colin.

"She's never out but she is a bit deaf," he said pressing the buzzer again.

A fit looking man with a dog walked up to the door making them stepped aside. "Evening guys. Getting colder now." He punched in a number followed by a buzzing sound and the door opened. They entered after him. He stopped inside and the dog growled. "Can I help you?"

"I'm Mina's cousin."

He turned without a word and started climbing the stairs. Mina's flat was the first on the left on the ground floor. Gordon knocked on the heavy mahogany door. It opened a little.

"Oh it's you Gordon come in."

The door widened to reveal a stooping small woman in her fifties who appeared to be recovering from an illness or perhaps was declining in health and closed behind them. Colin turned down his collar and gazed at the exuberant use of the colour pink on the walls. They followed her through to the sitting room where there was more of the same pink. Seated on a Victorian spoon back chair was a small woman leaning forward with her weight on a walking stick. Her fingers were long and thin accentuated by the delicacy of her skin with every vein clearly showing as she grasped the antler handle.

"Ishbel, you remember Gordon he's my mother's sisters boy?"

"Nice to meet you Ishbel this is an old friend of mine from the army, Colin."

"We've just eaten but I could get something for you if you would like," said Mina.

"No we're alright thanks Mina it's very nice to see you, are you well?"

"No, but never mind that, I'll make some tea. Would you like tea Ishbel?" Ishbel nodded.

She had been studying the two in a courteous but curious way. When Mina disappeared into the kitchen Ishbel cleared her throat.

"So your Netta's boy. Poor woman she had a terrible time with your father and all his shenanigans, she was well rid of him when he just disappeared into thin air...can anyone lead a blameless life? I doubt it. It depends on who makes the judgement eh? There was a knock on my door one day. It was a police woman who said she was looking for your father. So she came in and sat down and I looked into her eyes, she was a troubled soul. Something terrible had happened to her in recent times. Anyway she wanted me to help find him. Well I didn't know where he was but I knew that he would never be seen again. Mind you I wouldn't have told her if I had known. So Colin what ails ye?"

Colin smiled, "I was hoping to get some advice from you," Ishbel nodded.

Mina came back with a tray bearing a teapot covered with a knitted rabbit tea cosy, cups and saucers milk and sugar.

"Mina, Colin would like some advice can we use your front room?"

"Oh, I'm sure that will be Ok."

Mina wiped her hands on the pinny she was wearing and found a key in the oak tambour roll top desk. She unlocked the door and stood aside. It was dark due to the drawn heavy velvet curtains.

"Do you mind if I don't switch the light on Ishbel?"

"I understand Mina, Colin can you open the curtains a little please?" asked Ishbel.

The door closed behind them as light from a street lamp partially lit the room. Hanging from the centre of a plaster boss was a brass four light chandelier. Colin could just about make out a modest marble fire surround with a black cast-iron fireplace. Above was a gilt over-mantle mirror and to the left, a piano that had been left open revealing the ivory and ebony keys with sheet music, resting on the music stand. At either side of a four glass mantle timepiece were Georgian brass candlesticks with white candles. On the green patterned wallpaper hung pictures. Oils, watercolours and copperplate engravings were suspended from the picture rail. On the other side of the fireplace was an open Davenport desk and chair and next to it a small burr walnut credenza holding early pearl-ware china. Ishbel motioned Colin towards a circular pedestal table in the bay window covered with a brown damask material and they sat down opposite each other. She reached across with the palms of her hands facing up.

"I'm sorry I don't have any money," he said.

Ishbel cackled. "You don't need the gift to tell that you're stony broke," and wiggled her fingers. Colin responded by holding his hands out which were grasped by her bony fingers.

"Tell me why you're here."

"I'm looking for a man," he released a hand and reached for an inside pocket.

"No," she wiggled her fingers again and held his hand once more. "Tell me what happened."

When Colin had finished telling her about Jenny being shot and how he wanted to find Capello and kill him, he noticed she had closed her eyes. There was barely any pressure on his fingers now and he wondered if she was falling asleep.

"Mina's mother, Jean my sister died here in this room. It's been left as a shrine. It was a terrible shock to Mina though I knew Jean wasn't well. It was cancer. I couldn't bring myself to tell Mina." Ishbel sighed, "but there is a gateway a spiritual gateway in this room. I can feel it now." She opened her eyes. "I don't see souls of the dead. I don't communicate with the afterlife. Oh I think I could if I wanted to but I don't, RIP I say, leave the dead in peace. Colin you are a troubled man but a good man. Life has not been easy for you and yet you are a survivor. Always listen to the calmness that's inside your heart. You have asked for my advice and in asking you must carefully consider what I say and judge it as though it were your own thoughts."

"The Doctor says I suffer from Post-Traumatic Stress Disorder."

"Yes."

"I get angry occasionally for no reason."

"Yes."

"It's peaceful here...calm."

"Yes, you feel it too. Many people search for an inner calmness. It's not hard to find if you know where to look. You have seen some terrible things, things you may not wish to remember but life is short and the memory is long. Mayflies only live a few hours. If it had a memory it would be very short. Its only function is reproduction, a continuing cycle that has not been broken since the dawn of evolution. So you see everything is relative. Inside oneself, turning negativity into positivity can become an energy that will overcome anything."

Ishbel released his hands and looked out the window between the half drawn curtains. The cherry trees' branches now bare of leaves cast moving shadows from the mercury vapour street lamp, onto the dirty window. There was a barely audible sigh from her.

"Go home Colin. Forget about this Capello, his fate is sealed. Unlike you he has no future."

"Can you guarantee he'll get what he deserves?"

Ishbel laughed and shook her head. "No dearie the only guarantee I can give you is that my heart will keep beating until it stops. That the world will keep turning long after we're all dead and those questions that get answered, only create more questions, not better answers. What I am sure of is that there is only grief waiting if you continue your quest. Go home to Jenny and start a family. That's your future."

Capello walked along the narrow lane behind the warehouses and judged perfectly the right building. He fiddled with the lock until the door sprung open and climbed the stairs reaching the top. He pushed a door open revealing a derelict attic flat with two dormer windows strategically situated at the bend of the cul-de-sac. One with a view to the left of the end of the cul-de-sac and the other in the opposite direction, out to the main road. Empty boxes old chairs and damp walls from a roof leak were evidence of a property that appeared to have been abandoned. It was perfect for a stakeout. He pulled a green leather button back couch with the stuffing sticking out of it over to the window and made himself comfortable. He put down a bag of food and bottled water and opened his rucksack to find the night goggles. He guessed that if they were doing a watch on the van it would be a six hour shift starting at midnight in just a few minutes time. He took off the lens cap from the military grade AN/PVS-7B/D night goggles, flicked a switch and scanned the roof and windows opposite. It was possible that they may have had the same idea and be in the building next door. The dormer window consisted of three sliding sash windows with a centre and two angled frames of glass one at either side allowing him to see next door. He opened the window slightly and wedged an empty tin to stop it falling. He would be able to hear anyone coming and going. There was nothing stirring only the occasional vehicle passing on the main road.

He jumped cursing himself for falling asleep, had something woken him? He listened carefully and picked up the goggles checking the doorways in the street below but there was nothing. There was something scratching in the corner and there was a dragging sound close by. He switched on the infra-red light to see two rats trying to steal some food out of his bag. He moved his weight on the couch and they disappeared under a skirting board. He relaxed and wondered how many times he had staked out somewhere looking for someone, dozens probably. The last time was in a seedy run down part of San José, Costa Rica. He was sent to find a well-protected troublesome Nicaraguan who was attempting to foment an insurgency in the country. All that was required was patience lots of patience. A waning moon came from behind a cloud casting a pale blue light on him. It always took a few minutes for his eyes to adjust to the dark after looking through the goggles.

25

"Em I wish you would stop following me around you're like a lost puppy."

"That's quite a step up from a bad case of flu. Do you think I'm going to let you do a shift on your own? You should be at home. Oh my God what happens if you have the baby here? I've never even seen a birth I wouldn't know what to do. Anyway what would Bjørge say, you risking your life and your baby's, spending the night with me again."

They had been given permission to use the basement of a commercial photographer's unused darkroom immediately opposite Capello's building. It was full of relics of a pre-digital photography age. Large plate horizontal enlargers with bellows, a polished steel drum print drier, boxes of unopened ten by eight photographic paper, large developer and fixing dishes with the unmistakeable smell of pungent sodium thiosulfate still apparent. They were watching three monitors. One showed the van and the other two the approaches left and right. Iona had got her appetite back and seemed to be constantly eating.

"Does the smell of that fixer not put you off food?" asked Emlyn playing with a clockwork timer.

She shook her head. "Smells a bit like pickled onions."

"Seriously Iona I worry about you."

"Phew, I'm hot it's stuffy in here. I don't like not having any windows." Her face was flushed as she finished off the sausage roll. "I have to find the loo." She stood up and waddled off.

Emlyn looked at his watch, five o'clock and another hour to go. It had gone too fast. He liked being near Iona, there was a definite chemistry between them, what kind he wasn't sure. He sighed and a great sadness gripped him. Iona came back and sat down but he just stared at the monitors. He knew he couldn't compete with Bjørge. Iona sensed his mood and touched his shoulder.

"Em, I am very fond of you, we've been through a lot together and I do owe you a great deal and I am grateful. Possibly if I wasn't pregnant and there was no Bjørge, things could have been different between us. But my future is with him and our baby and that won't change. The reason I'm saying this is because

I know that somewhere out there is a girl who's waiting to meet someone like you."

"You don't understand. There's a cosmic connection binding the two of us together, maybe not as...lovers but this has all been pre-ordained by some powerful force like, God...or a novelist." They both jumped when the timer went off unexpectedly. "Sorry about that." He put it down. "I was destined to meet you. It was meant to be. The chance of face recognition cameras flagging you up so quickly was extremely remote. I was destined to save your life. The puff of smoke from the parked van could have been anything yet I reacted. I'm amazed you can't see it."

"I can, kind of but I'm not really into the whole of someone's future being already set in concrete and that we're like ants forced to obey the laws of destiny. Look I don't normally bring this up but I have a PhD in Philosophy and Psychology. So you should really be calling me Doctor McCallum anyway the point I'm making is that we are all masters of our own fortune and subsequently responsible for everything that we do. Otherwise you could have a murderer's defence being that it wasn't him, it was written in the stars."

"I know you're a Doctor I've read your file remember?" Iona nodded. "Ok well Doctor McCallum I want you to promise me something."

"What?"

"No what's, I want you to give me a solemn promise."

"Don't be soft in the head I can't just give you a promise until I know what it is."

"Ok, when the baby is born I want you to promise me you'll name it...

"...Emlyn?" I can't do that Bjørge would..."

"Not my name...I want you to name her Destiny."

"Em don't be daft whoever heard of a boy called Destiny."

She leaned back in her chair and studied his expression. It was easy to read his feelings and she always seemed to be hurting them.

"Please?"

"Oh alright. I will promise you this. In the unlikely event that it's a girl I will consider calling her Destiny."

Emlyn took her hand and kissed it. "See," he said with a smile. She gazed at him wondering what he would have been like...when her text alert pinged.

Cold wind flitted under the propped open sash window fluttering the torn and faded curtain. A hint of light appeared under the uniform layer of low cloud to the east signalling a new day. As the sun rose above the horizon a shaft of red light illuminated the base of an extensive Stratos cloud formation and reflected an intense crimson glow downwards. Capello was taken off guard and quickly put the cap over the lens of the goggles to protect it. At the same time he heard someone walking along the pavement from the main street. It was a tall blond woman in a dark trouser suit carrying a backpack. He watched as she approached the block opposite and entered. His heart rate increased forcing him to calm it down, take control. He watched hardly breathing. The door opposite opened again. He breathed out and whispered. "*Zas.*" He left everything and raced downstairs knocking over boxes and slipping on several stairs to reach the back door. He ran down the narrow lane to the end and stopped, breathing heavily. He peered round the corner hoping they weren't going to walk towards him and as luck would have it, they were approaching. He retreated into the shadows and held his breath.

"Em, where do you think you're going you don't have to walk me back." The door closed with a click. "Look at that sky its blood red."

"I'm not listening to you anymore, you're...thrawn," he said.

"That's a Scottish word," she said giving a mock clap.

"I know," he said exasperated.

"I'm hungry."

"You've been eating all night."

"For breakfast."

Emlyn started singing softly. "Iona, you're breaking my heart you're shaking my confidence daily, oh Iona I'm down on my knees I'm begging you..."

"Shut up Em, people are sleeping." She turned her head away from him trying to stifle a laugh passing the narrow lane hiding Capello in the shadows. "Who was that supposed to be anyway?"

"Simon and Garfunkel of course. You need to get out more."

Iona stopped out of breath. "Wait." She put a hand against the wall and looked down. "I don't feel good."

"No wonder with all that rubbish you've been eating. Come on you can lean against me if it doesn't go against your principles." She allowed him to put an arm around her waist.

It was easy for Capello to follow the pre-occupied couple at a safe distance along the main road passing one alley then another road before they turned right up a similar cobbled lane. He stopped at the corner weighing up his options which were limited. In his hurry he had left the Heckler & Koch pistol behind but it was better to plan ahead than be rushed into an unknown situation. Just at a point where the couple were going to disappear round a corner they crossed the road and entered a recessed door. Capello turned and walked back to the narrow lane, found the rear door and climbed the stairs to the attic flat. He looked out the window and noticed that a car had parked on the corner of the main road and the cobbled lane. He put on his shoulder holster, gathered all his things together and packed them away into a rucksack. He looked around to make sure it was left just as he had found it, closed the door and went downstairs. Reaching the end of the alleyway he stopped and looked left but the car that was parked had gone. He reached his car that had a parking ticket on the windscreen wiper. He cursed his carelessness removing the ticket. It was just as well that this was his last job he was getting too old. He started the car and drove it up the cobbled road passed the Intel HQ, negotiated the bend and out of sight of the building did a three point turn. He parked on the bend sticking out just enough to see the comings and goings.

26

Images of a registration plate came into focus through a pair of Leitz binoculars. Lewis Sebastian Digby couldn't believe his luck.

"Grace this is crazy, Iona should not be here never mind doing field work," said Emlyn.

Iona came waddling through from the toilet. "My back's killing me and it's getting harder to walk properly."

"You're right Emlyn."

"What's going on guys? Phew I have to sit down."

"Iona I think it's time for you to go home."

"I suppose you're right, excuse me I have to go to the loo again."

"Something tells me our plan is not working," said Grace. "James if nothing happens during Jacqui's shift pack up the equipment then drive the van round here and into the basement, ok? Here's the keys it's time to go." James threw on his anorak and left. "Have you eaten, Emlyn?"

"I had something earlier, I'm not hungry."

"Love does that to you." Emlyn looked at her in surprise. "You can't hide anything from Grace I've been through it all and back again, twice. Just don't mess up Iona's life Emlyn, she's a nice girl."

"Believe me, I would never do that."

"Good, have you thought about what you want to do now?"

"Well when you feel you don't need me anymore I'll go back to Wales. You know I phoned my mother yesterday and she didn't even know I was supposed to be dead. I thought she would be surprised to hear from me and all I got was an earful for not keeping in touch. Grace can I ask you something? You know I'm crazy about Iona and the last thing I want to do is cause her any problems but how do you know that her future is with Bjørge? I mean, I know she likes me...quite a bit actually...nothing's happened though."

"No you don't. I'm not giving advice on a ménage et trois."

There was a door alert. Grace looked at the monitor to see Jacqui swiping her card and then the door burst open and she went sprawling across the floor.

Everyone stood still in shock. Capello closed the door, both arms by his side one hand holding the pistol as Iona walked out of the toilets.

"Oh my, I'm very uncomfortable Grace. You know it wouldn't surprise me if it was getting..."

"Come on in Iona join the party."

Jacqui made to get up. "What's your name?" he asked.

"Jacqui."

"Well Jacqui stay on the floor with your hands where I can see them. Llewellyn nice to see you again. Grace, tut tut your security is very lax."

Emlyn went over to Iona and stood between her and Capello.

"Grace, we are professionals and I hope you understand that there is absolutely nothing personal in what will happen."

"Work for us Capello, you could do worse."

He laughed and shook his head. "That is extremely gracious of you and under any other circumstances I would be only too glad to accept your kind offer however I am not yet the master of my own destiny, soon though, soon and now to business."

He raised the pistol and shot Grace in the middle of her forehead leaving a neat hole. She fell to the ground without a sound. Jacqui reached for the pistol in her shoulder holster and caught a bullet in the chest that pierced her heart. Her head went sideways and her body relaxed. Sightless eyes stared at Iona.

"Now Iona you wanted to know why Jane was so upset with you..."

"No," she replied.

"Well I can tell you now..."

"No."

"You see, she thought you had stolen clearance pass-codes, usernames, operation manuals, lists of agents active and non-active and a network map of all the servers used by GCHQ, MI5 and SIS. However it probably won't come as a surprise to you to learn, that I have it."

"Stop."

"So Jane was wrong, she isn't wrong very often but her judgement must have been clouded because, well maybe she saw you as a threat. An up and coming intelligent analyst with a PhD made her very uncomfortable. She was only too pleased to believe the worst, an Achilles heel I'm afraid. So now you both know, sorry Llewellyn. I have to do some house cleaning and then I'll be off."

"Don't be an animal Capello, Iona is close to giving birth. There's nothing professional about killing a pregnant woman."

"Ha, love. It's a luxury agents cannot afford. It clouds the judgement, increases the options, never a good thing. So you die together, it's poetic don't you think?" He raised the pistol and pointed it at them. A smile came to his face as Emlyn shielded Iona. "You don't even know what kind of pistol this is Llewellyn. Heckler & Koch USP? No didn't think so it fires a .357 round that will go right through you and Iona and probably another two people if they were behind you. It saddens me I have to admit but needs must."

He raised the pistol again. Iona put her arms round Emlyn holding him tight and they both closed their eyes waiting for death. The silenced H&K coughed and caught Emlyn on the chest. Iona stepped back and screamed as he fell on the floor with a gasp.

"Strange," Capello shrugged lowering his pistol. "Up until now you must have had a charmed life, have you named your baby?"

"Destiny," she said with tears running down her cheeks.

"Destiny, unusual name. Well goodbye Iona and goodbye Destiny there will be no one left to shed tears."

Iona closed her eyes and protectively placed her arms in front of the baby. He raised the pistol and took aim and almost at the same time there was a curious sharp ping sound. Capello fell to the ground. Outside sounds filtered through a neat hole in the window with cracks emanating from it. Blood was welling around Capello's head. Iona opened her eyes and looked at the carnage in front of her. Jacqui, Grace, Emlyn and now Capello. She searched for her phone and was just about to dial when Digby burst through the door and stopped.

"Put the phone down." Iona placed it on the desk next to her. Digby looked around the large room and approached Capello. "Do not do anything foolish for your baby's sake," he said without looking at her. "What a mess, whatever have you been up to Mr Capello?" He checked Capello's pockets found the drive and stood up with it in his hand. "Move away from the desk." Iona did as she was asked.

"My friend is injured he needs a Doctor." Digby picked up her phone dropped it on the floor and stamped on it.

"Do not do anything for the next two minutes, do not phone or leave do nothing. Believe me it would be a very bad idea." Then he left.

With difficulty and tears in her eyes, Iona kneeled down next to Emlyn and supported his head on her lap just as James arrived with mouth open. He dialled the emergency number and she took the phone from him. She explained where they were and what had happened. Emlyn was unconscious and losing blood. Iona ended the call. She had cheated death once again because of Emlyn. His eyes were closed and she couldn't tell if he was breathing. There was a lot of blood on the ground. She looked at the phone in her hand and dialled a number putting it to her ear.

"Mum, Mum I love you..."

The armed response unit arrived and fanned out checking the floor. Then it was clear for the medics who came forward to Iona. They helped her to her feet and put Emlyn on a stretcher and out to the ambulance.

"Where are you darling

"I'm going off to hospital."

"Are you alright?" asked the medic.

"Yes I need a scan just to make sure the baby is alright. Mum it's so nice to hear your voice..."

"...Let's get you off to hospital."

"Call Bjørge, Mum."

Jane Caddish looked at the text she had just received. '*Capello dead, item recovered.*' There was no sense of victory or triumphalism, no job-well-done or relief it was just the end of another chapter in the book of life. Earlier there had been a text from her line manager requesting her resignation. The text, a clear intention to denigrate the message by the use of the messenger wasn't lost on her. Much better just quietly leaving than being potentially embroiled in a messy inquiry and it could easily be put down to yet another wave of redundancy requests. At least that was the implied hint. She looked at the TV news on her monitor but her mind was miles away. Something was gnawing inside her that she couldn't ignore.

The establishment would look after her of course in their own way. An excellent pension, a directorship in a communications company or a trusteeship on a large charity, there were scores of ways she could be quietly bought off. And as a result there would be no question of her being a scapegoat because in her privileged world culpability was irrelevant. One thing, perhaps the only thing that the civil service was good at was protecting its own. She knew much about a lot of people and even those who she didn't have anything on feared that she might. No doubt there would be inquiry after inquiry the results of which would be lost in the labyrinthine shelves of civilservicedom. She wasn't afraid of death she wasn't averse to shrugging off the responsibility of collateral damage as a result of her decisions. There were always swings and roundabouts to balance out every situation. Nor did it bother her having to live with the responsibility for innocent deaths.

But a life outside the firm? That was different. She had given her life to GCHQ, there was no other partner but now she felt betrayed. She had slavishly obeyed the orders from above and when the political winds shifted she was exposed. What destroyed her most was that GCHQ was her life. It was her partner her best friend and such as it was, her leisure time spent in the senior management restaurant or in the fitness and games room. It was everything. It was her reason for being. People who thought that they knew her believed she was tough and she was, but sometimes the toughness was shell deep and just as fragile. When she took on the post she knew it was a poisoned chalice but she thought she had the antidote. Now it had lost its effectiveness. Her phone rang, it was Colleen Bentsen.

"Ma'am I hear you're leaving"

"Yes, I'm being made redundant."

"Redundant? I don't understand it they need you. Anyway I just thought I'd let you know that I'm sorry you'll be going."

"Thanks Colleen."

That was only the second time she had called her by her first name. The first time was when she accidentally bumped into her in the town.

"By the way there's more to it than being made redundant. Um there is going to be an inquiry. If you're asked any questions," she paused, "just answer them truthfully."

27

Alison Holt was fidgeting in her studio chair and in the process her earpiece fell out. She swore.

"Live in ten Alison."

She shuffled her script and satisfied put on her best broadcasting smile.

"Good afternoon you are watching the 24 Hour News channel with Alison Holt and breaking news the acting First Minister of Scotland is about to give a very important statement to MSP's at Holyrood. Speculation has been mounting as to the outcome of talks between Constance Black and the Prime Minister. The expectation is that a deal has been reached after the talks brokered by Raknar Aalto President of the European Parliament. Strict security and secrecy has surrounded the discussions and unusually there has been no details released so far. However the terms of the deal which it is hoped will end the conflict will undoubtedly be in her statement. It has been a bloody conflict with many people dying and injured. Businesses have suffered, tourism figures have dropped and North Sea oil production is in virtual paralysis. Mass demonstrations and national strikes were planned along with tax payment strikes. The question is on everyone's lips will Keating's government concede power to Scotland and under which circumstances, but first we're going over to Downing Street live to hear from Charles Keating."

"It has always been the duty and responsibility of my government to protect its citizens. There was a very real likelihood that the fabric of civil society in Scotland was in real danger of collapse and above everything else, order had to be maintained. That is why it was imperative to implement some very strict measures that were put in place where necessary. I am not going to pretend that this was in any way ideal or the answer to a very difficult set of circumstances. Now it is time for reconciliation, for rebuilding trust between the two nations for working together for a new future. That is why I have decided and that both parties have concluded that the best way forward is for Scotland to have home rule. The details of which have been agreed. Now the acting First Minister Constance Black will be speaking to her parliament shortly and she will be giving more details. Finally I would like to say this to the people of Scotland everything that was done by this government was done in good faith. Let us progress and flourish together as equal partners and build a better tomorrow for all of us living on this island."

"That was Prime Minister Keating and with me is political editor Hugh Platt, Hugh a significant change in direction almost a volte-face, what do you make of the Prime Minister's statement."

"Well it's been coming. The only surprise is that this hasn't happened sooner. Keating has been under intense pressure from all quarters indeed he appears to have been almost isolated in his policies towards Scotland. Don't forget the warnings that came from America, Canada and quite a lot of other commonwealth countries not to mention Europe especially after what happened in Stirling."

"Do you think that was the turning point?"

"The turning point was undoubtedly the Stirling massacre and the disquiet and alarm felt within his own party was making it impossible for him to keep a lid on it. It simply couldn't continue and I think that at the back of many minds after Stirling was, what will Scotland do next? It could so easily have turned into a bloody conflict engulfing both countries. It's interesting to note that he was willing for Constance Black to give the details of the agreement perhaps that is the early signs of rapprochement. It'll be fascinating to hear what she has to say."

"Will this be enough to defuse tensions north of the border?"

"Well that's a very good question after all this is not full sovereignty that's been offered and Scotland will still be part of the UK. So Ms Black firstly has to be satisfied with the deal struck and then she has to persuade her government and parliament and then she has to persuade fellow Scots. That won't be easy especially for those who have lost loved ones."

"For now thank you Hugh and joining us in the studio is Professor Karl Hofler from Glasgow University, Professor Hofler do you think that the tone is conciliatory enough?"

"Well perhaps at this early stage but for Scotland's acting First Minister to feel that there could be a solution in what was proposed is remarkable enough. This isn't even close to full sovereignty so like Hugh it'll be fascination to hear what the detail is."

"If I twisted your arm could you give us your thoughts of what might be in the detail?"

"Well Constance was Deputy Leader and a very able and intelligent woman she is too who will make a fine First Minister who knows perhaps Scotland's' first Prime Minister. There must have been substantial concessions made that would persuade her to accept such a deal and..."

"...I'm sorry Professor we're going over now live to Holyrood to hear Constance Black the acting First Minister. Are we?" she said to the gallery. "They're not quite ready for us...no well while we wait for Constance Black, some other breaking news. There have been reports of a shooting in Leith. The police have said that two office workers have died and one taken to hospital in a critical condition. A third body is believed to be that of the gunman and the police have issued this photograph to try and establish his identity."

The photograph of Capello appeared on the screen. Colin stared at it in astonishment. There was no doubting it was Capello. "Ishbel was right," he said closing his eyes and starting to shake.

"...The police say they are not looking for anyone else in connection with the incident. Now we can go over to Holyrood..."

"Who's Ishbel?"

Jenny had been moved to a private room in the hospital. He opened his eyes. She was still looking weak.

"I don't even know her last name. She's a seer, a Highland seer. She helped me a lot."

"Are you ok?" asked Jenny.

He smiled. "Absolutely fine. I've got something for you."

"Shush I want to hear what Constance Black is saying."

"It won't wait."

Jenny looked at Colin and turned down the sound of the television mounted on the wall.

"You're looking so much better," he said

"I feel stronger every day."

"Close your eyes."

Colin reached into his pocket and took out a ring. He took her hand and dropped it into her open palm. She opened her eyes in surprise.

"It's beautiful. Colin how could you possible afford an engagement ring like that?"

"It's Mums she wanted you to have it."

It had three diamonds on a gold band. She hugged him with a beaming smile kissed him and turned up the sound.

"...Friends, whichever part of the political spectrum you come from there is no doubting the coming together of all parties in condemning the tragedy that occurred in Stirling, the bombing of the American Diner and all those others who have lost their lives. I know that everyone's sympathies will be with the families and friends of those who have lost loved ones. Their deaths will not be in vain. There were will be a judicial enquiry into the Stirling massacre and those responsible will be prosecuted. Those guilty parties will be found and punished but this is a time when we must look forward and embrace the future. I have had extensive talks with Prime Minister Keating and I believe a solution has been found. With immediate effect Scotland will have home rule with a programme over a period of ten years to make the transition to full sovereignty. Today is the historic beginning of a journey towards a free Scotland. A future Scotland that will have the power to remove inequalities in education, in health and in the pocket. The Scottish Government together will seek radical progressive policies that will enrich not impoverish our people. We have published a document entitled 'Scotland's Future' that sets out a timetable for the transition and how it will affect everyone."

Emlyn was heavily sedated. His eyes followed Bjørge as he came in and sat next to him on the bed. Bjørge looked awkward, studied his finger nails and cleared his throat. He had no idea how it came about that a gunman would run amok trying to kill Iona and Emlyn. Like most things with Iona he just had to be patient. She would tell him in her own good time.

Emlyn watched Bjørge and a pang of annoyance broke through his befuddled state. Here was his bumbling rival that he could not compete with. Things might have changed had he made love to Iona that first night. He was never any good at reading female signals, far too much the gentleman. Life wasn't fair.

"Iona's in maternity. How are you feeling?"

"*Bumbling buffoon.*" Emlyn mumbled.

Bjørge held up his hand. "Don't try to talk. The Doctor said I could see you and she also said you shouldn't exert yourself. I heard what you did and I can't thank you enough. I'm told that the bullet hit the third rib on the right which deflected it upwards away from the heart into the muscle of your shoulder. The broken rib punctured the lung, you're very lucky to be alive. The Doctor said that if the bullet had missed the rib it would have gone through the heart and kept on...hitting Iona. You seem to be making a habit of saving her life. She wanted me to see you, well I wanted to see you too of course, to thank you. The midwife says they are going to induce labour in case there are problems. Emlyn I know that you love Iona and I know that she is very fond of you and..."

"*Oblivious oyk.*" He mumbled again.

Emlyn closed his eyes with the hint of a smile. The morphine was taking him to another place. He tried to concentrate on what Bjørge was saying. What was the point of replying? What had happened at HQ was a blur, he didn't even remember being shot, just the surprise of lying on the ground not being able to get up and then nothing. He didn't want to listen to what Bjørge was saying anymore. It was over, his adventure with Iona had come to an end. He knew he was going to be alright at least that's what the Doctor said and so what, it didn't matter too much. He wasn't caring about anything. The truth was that he hadn't felt this intense euphoria since he was a child. He wished that Bjørge would just go away and let him enjoy it in peace.

"Mr Tennfjord, Iona is asking for you," said the nurse.

"Oh thanks. We'll talk again Emlyn. If there's anything you need just let me know."

Bjørge arrived when Iona was pushing. She was breathless red-faced and sweating. He pulled over the chair from the window placing it next to the bed and held her hand. She smiled apprehensively. The midwife and nurse were making a fuss of her knowing it was her first. You could tell they worked together a lot as a team.

"How's Emlyn?" she asked.

"Hard to tell. He seemed to be in another world. Kept mumbling something but I couldn't make it out. The Doctors say he'll be fine and very

very lucky to be alive. You too. He didn't say much, probably doped to the eyeballs."

"Push Iona come on. Push," said the midwife.

"I am. You try it it's not so easy."

"I've got three and believe me none of them were easy."

"Bjørge I must see Em before I go."

"Push."

"I don't think that's a good idea."

"Push."

"I'm PUSHING! Why do you think it's not a good idea?"

"Clean break, best thing."

"Ok rest."

"Don't be ridiculous Bjørge I have to thank him and anyway I want him to see the baby. You

wouldn't be jealous by any chance?"

"No I'm not."

"Iona concentrate, push."

"Yes...you...ARE."

"Iona, again."

"Maybe a little," he said.

"Nearly there."

"I love you."

Bjørge could see the top of the baby's head. He gripped her hand and then the head came out and the baby began crying.

"Iona it's a girl," said the midwife.

She was wrapped in a towel and handed to Iona who was exhausted and happy. "Thank God it's a girl," she said.

"Girl eh?" said Bjørge smiling from ear to ear. Now what shall we name her how about

Ragnhild or Synnøve, I know Ingeborg?"

Iona leaned back cradling her baby with a knowing smile and said, "We're going to call her Destiny."

End